Great Snoring Stegosaurs!

Written and Illustrated by

Scott E. Sutton

Sutton Studios, Inc. • scottesutton.com

ISBN: 978-0-9851061-4-0

Sutton Studios, Inc.
Visit us online at scottesutton.com

MEGA ULTRA EXTREMELY TOP SECRET
FOR SCIENCE TEAM EYES ONLY!
VIOLATORS WILL BE SENT TO JAIL – FOREVER!

The official time tunnel back to the Age of Dinosaurs Science Team is ...

Me, Benjamin Montgomery or Banjo – author, researcher and artist.

My best friend, Lee Wong – he is the science guy and does planning and stuff.

Samantha Burke, my cousin who lives in our guest house – she is our computer person and security.

Dino, my Chow Chow dog – he is in charge of guarding and security and attacking.

Bootsey, who is Sam's cat – he helps with security and he is an expert escape cat.

SCIENCE LOG #5

Hi, Banjo Montgomery here.

This Science Log will bring you up to date on the BIGGEST DISCOVERY EVER. A few months ago, my dog Dino had something REALLY WEIRD happen. His doggie door, in our garage, mysteriously turned into the entrance to a TIME TUNNEL going back to THE AGE OF DINOSAURS!

This tunnel forms because two floating robot aliens fly their time-traveling space ship over my house when they go back in time.

Their names are ARBEE and ZINZU and they are like a race of alien librarians. They are studying the ancient history of nearby planets, including Earth. They are from the planet Izikzah, one hundred light-years from Earth. Arbee and Zinzu are good aliens, not EVIL ones. We made them promise NOT to invade the world and they have not done it so far, so that is good.

ARBEE

Me, Lee and my Chow Chow dog Dino put together a Science Team to investigate. Later Samantha Burke and her cat joined our team. We have been helping Arbee and Zinzu study real live DINOSAURS. We go back every two weeks when Arbee travels back to different times.

We have not told ANYBODY about this because you cannot bring stuff from a past time to this time. That includes photos or videos because it ALL DISAPEARS and if we told people about this without proof they would say "Hey, you kids are CRAZY! Ha, ha, ha, now go clean your rooms."

TOP SECRET – SCIENCE LOG – DO NOT READ!

We saw some T-Rexes, some Triceratops, Diplodocus, Pteranodons, and a bunch of awesome dinosaurs, and a lot of them have FEATHERS on them. Some of these things were like giant BIRDS.

They used to call the time when dinosaurs lived 'The Age of Reptiles'. Reptiles ... no way, these things are NOT REPTILES.

It should be called "The Age of Giant, Monster, Killer BIRDS"!

IF YOU DO NOT BELIEVE ME, THEN YOU ARE NOT PART OF THE OFFICIAL SCIENCE TEAM SO GET OFF MY COMPUTER RIGHT NOW OR I WILL SUE YOU AND YOU WILL GO TO JAIL!

Here is what happened to us on our last trip back in time ...

We went through the doggie door time tunnel to Arbee's starship and it was over 100 million years in the past. We were starving, so Arbee made some fried chicken and it was SO good. Then we went to study a dinosaur called DEINONYCHUS. Deinonychus is like a North American type of meat-eating dinosaur called Velociraptor. Only they are BIGGER AND MEANER!

They hunt in packs like wolves and are real smart, too. They also have feathers on them. We found a pack of these things ... well ... they sort of found us.

Then all of a sudden – BAM – they attacked us. The leader Deinonychus stole some of my fried chicken, too. We escaped back to Arbee's space ship but the Deinonychus pack followed us and somehow SNUCK ONTO THE SHIP! They chased after us all over the starship. It was like something out of a Hollywood movie but it was WORSE because it was REAL!

Me and Dino got mad and we attacked the Deinonychus but we both got wounded by their claws. The Deinonychus teeth and claws have some kind of poison on them, only this poison will not let your cuts heal so you BLEED TO DEATH! Totally gross.

Arbee and Zinzu had to fly us back to their home planet, Izikzah, to take us to an alien hospital and this alien doctor cured us just in time, or we would have DIED... FOREVER!

Izikzah is a cool planet. All their people have floating robot bodies like Arbee and Zinzu. Their planet is a center for knowledge and education. Most of their world is libraries and universities.

ROBOT ALIEN PEOPLE from PLANET IZIKZAH

Anyway, it turns out that the Deinonychus pack came on the ship because they wanted more FRIED CHICKEN. So, Arbee used fried chicken to get the dinosaurs out of the space ship. I think this is weird because these things are like birds so they are like eating themselves from the future ... which I think is CREEPY .... and weird.

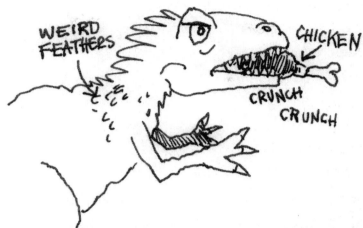

IF PEOPLE TELL YOU DINOSAURS ARE STUPID, DO NOT BELIEVE THEM! They are smarter than you think. I know because I have seen them in action!

It has been two weeks, so me and Lee and Dino are going back to see Arbee. Sam is already there. She goes back more because she is helping Arbee do stuff.

I do not know what dinosaurs we are going to study this time, but I sure hope it is not psycho Deinonychus because DYING is a bad thing!

End of Science Log #5
Benjamin Montgomery
Author and artist

Oh ... if I get eaten and die, Mom and Dad you have my permission to read this.

Chapter One
ATTACK OF THE BIRDOSAURS

Dogs, like people, have some very bad days during their short lives and Dino – Banjo Montgomery's big furry Chow-Chow dog – had just survived the WORST three days he could remember ... EVER!

"The last three days were WORSE than the time I was sprayed right in the face by a SKUNK that I was chasing because I thought it was a CAT," thought Dino. "They gave me five baths and they STILL would not let me in the house because I smelled too SKUNKY."

"The last three days were EVEN WORSE than the time I went into Mrs. Montgomery's closet and chewed up a bunch of her expensive shoes," thought Dino. "She was so mad at me that she said, 'I am going to send that FUZZ BALL back to the DOG POUND where he came from.'"

"If I had to spend one more day trapped by those huge cow-lizards then I would have been ... one ... DEAD ... DOG," he thought.

Luckily, Dino was now safely back on board the time-traveling starship belonging to Arbee and Zinzu – two alien librarians doing research on the ancient history of planets in this part of the galaxy.

The information they collected from their research was added to in the huge database at the Universal Central Library on their home planet, Izikzah.

The library is there so that teachers, researchers and students from all over the galaxy can learn more about it.

When Dino was rescued he was a mess. So, Arbee cleaned him up and fed him two big bowls of his favorite food … steak.

"This is the first food I have eaten in THREE DAYS!" thought Dino. "I was so hungry that I tried eating some fern leaves and bushes but they tasted like … LEAVES and they just made me throw up. That proves dogs are NOT vegetarians. We need to eat cows or squirrels or chickens or even rabbits. Rabbits are good."

After he had finished his food, poor, tired Dino went and laid on a warm bed that Arbee had made for him in the corner of the starship's small kitchen next to the ship's control center on the bridge.

Dino was so tired that he slept without even dreaming. Sleeping next to Dino was Samantha Burke's cat, Bootsey, who had helped rescue him.

Sleeping on the other side of Dino was a strange alien guest. This alien guest had saved Dino and helped him escape a pack of huge meat-eating dinosaurs.

While Dino slept, Banjo Montgomery, his best friend Lee Wong, and Banjo's cousin Samantha Burke, were meeting with the starship's captain, Arbee, and the ship's second in command, Zinzu.

Banjo was finally smiling for the first time in days. His thick, red hair was a mess and he had dark circles under his eyes from not sleeping.

"Man, I thought Dino had been eaten or trampled for sure," said Banjo, shaking his head. "This has been the WORST three days I can remember ... EVER."

"Yeah, I can't even believe we found him" added Lee. "That dog is totally lucky to be alive."

"Well, he is safe now," Arbee sighed, "but now we have some VERY serious problems and we had better fix them fast or we may never leave this time and place ... ALIVE."

Dino's near death adventure started three days earlier when Arbee flew him, Banjo, Lee and Sam in one of the starship's shuttle craft out to do some research on a new and very odd looking dinosaur.

"Hang on," said Arbee. "We are landing near that herd of Stegosaurs."

Stegosaurus was a large four-legged plant-eater with a row of tall overlapping fins or plates going down the middle of its back, and it had four sharp spikes at the end of its tail.

The ship landed quietly and everyone stepped out on to the fern covered ground...

"All right everyone, we must approach the herd carefully and quietly, "whispered Arbee.

"Yeah we don't want to get stuck in a stampede," grumbled Lee. "We were caught in one once and we were nearly smashed like ... tiny ... little ... bugs."

"Do all of you have flash marbles and sling shots?" asked Arbee

"Yeah, we do," they all answered.

"Good, we must always be on guard out here," said Arbee. "All right, let us all move in closer ... slowly."

Banjo and Sam crept in so close to the huge dinosaurs that they could touch them. The Stegosaurs were very calm. They were not used to humans and their smells did not frighten them.

"Hey, look at this," whispered Sam. She had picked some ferns and was feeding them to a giant Stegosaurus. The dinosaur was eagerly eating the branches right out of her hand. "It's like feeding an animal at the zoo."

"Look at the size of that cow-lizard," thought Dino. "It's as big as a BUS." Dino sniffed one of the Stegosaurs. It went – SNORF – and snorted on him. "Same to you spiky tail cow-lizard and you have cow breath, too."

Banjo quietly broke off some fern branches and fed another Stegosaurus. "He is eating mine too. This is awesome," he said quietly.

Lee was standing further back. "Should you guys be doing this?" he said in a loud whisper. "I don't think you guys should be doing this. These things are wild animals you know and you never know what they are going to do, plus they are huge ... and they have those spiky tails ... and they are HUGE."

Just then many of the Stegosaurs made grunting noises and moved away from the Science Team turning their spiked tails toward them.

"Move back everyone," said Arbee. "Back away from their tails. Something is scaring them."

Dino heard the – CRACK– of a branch behind them. He turned around and "Gerrrrrrr, arf, arf," he barked a warning but it was too late. Dino saw some sort of feathered dinosaur leap into the air and – THUMP – land on the backpack Banjo was wearing.

"AAAAH," he screamed and fell to the ground trying to knock the creature off of him.

In an instant Dino charged in and grabbed the dinosaur by the throat and shook it hard, breaking its neck instantly. It flopped on the ground in a cloud of feathers. It was dead.

"Good boy, come on Dino," yelled Banjo, as he got to his feet and ran over to where the rest of his friends were. He grabbed his sling shot and loaded it, ready to fight.

"Look out." yelled Lee. "Here comes a whole bunch of those things." Lee also had his sling shot ready.

From out of the nearby forest of pine trees and tall ferns came a swarm of bird-like dinosaurs that were about three feet tall and covered with brown, white and black feathers. They had sharp teeth and claws and they were definitely meat-eaters looking for something to kill and eat.

The 'Birdosaurs' moved at lightning speed and were just about to pounce on the Science Team when Arbee yelled, "SHOOT them NOW!"

Sam, Banjo and Lee fired at their attackers – TWACK, TWACK, TWACK – the flash marbles flew towards their targets and – FLASH, FLASH, FLASH – they silently exploded with a blinding blue light.

Seven or eight of the Birdosaurs dropped instantly to the ground. They would be knocked out for fifteen minutes.

Arbee had given the Science Team members the flash marbles to defend themselves. But today it was not enough.

"RELOAD, HURRY!" yelled Banjo, but the Birdosaurs came at them too fast. Banjo managed to shoot one more but he could not reload before he was surrounded by two of the dinosaurs.

"Arf, arf, arf!" barked Dino. The angry dog was held back by his leash but was lunging and keeping the Birdosaurs from biting at Banjo.

Arbee, whose floating electronic body was faster than any human, was counter-attacking with lightning speed and zapping the charging creatures where ever he could.

"Get ... away ... from ... ME!" yelled Sam as she smacked one over and over again with her camera – WHAP, WHAP, WHAP – until it ran off with blood dripping from its mouth.

"I can't load fast enough," screamed Lee. "Hi-yah, hah, hi-yah ... let go my shoe stupid BIRD." Lee used the only defense he had ... his hands and feet. It took three kicks to the face and a punch to the eye of the Birdosaur but he finally drove the beast away, but not before it almost bit off Lee's shoe!

Banjo was still surrounded by two of the dinosaurs. He took off his backpack and used it as a weapon –BAPP – he knocked one back into the bushes. The second one leaped into the air and was about to dig its sharp claws into Banjo's chest.

Dino saw what the Birdosaur was about to do and performed an old Chow Chow dog trick. In an instant he slipped out of his collar so he could really fight.

He jumped up and caught the dinosaur by the skin on its stomach and slammed it to the ground and fiercely shook it. It screamed with pain. Dino shook it back and forth and threw it into a clump of ferns. It ran, limping into the forest as fast as it could and so did the rest of the Birdosaur pack.

And THAT is when it happened ...

Dino had never been this angry in his life.

The Birdosaurs took off running into the forest realizing that they could not eat these creatures ... but that was not good enough for Dino. He ran after them as fast as he could.

"DINO, STOP!" yelled Banjo "COME BACK!" Banjo ran as fast as possible after Dino, but before he got too far, two huge Ceratosaurs burst from the forest right in front of him, "REROWWW!"

The big meat-eaters were attracted by all the noise and came running to see if they could get a free meal.

The Ceratosaurs made the situation go from very bad to … a lot worse.

"LOOK OUT BANJO!" warned Arbee.

One of the Ceratosaurs saw Banjo and went straight for him.

"YAAAAA," screamed Banjo as he skidded to a stop, landing on his butt in the dirt.

The hungry dinosaur tried to bite Banjo's leg. Banjo quickly rolled to the right and – SNAP – went the jaws of the Ceratosaur closing like a steel trap, missing Banjo by only a few inches.

It was Sam's quick thinking that probably saved Banjo's life.

She grabbed a rock, ran towards the dinosaur and yelled, "GET OUT OF HERE." Then "umph," she threw the rock as hard as she could and –THUD – hit the Ceratosaur right on the nose.

SNORT – the dinosaur backed away just long enough for Lee to fire a shot with his sling shot – FLASH. The first Ceratosaur went down.

Banjo scrambled out of the way just before he was crushed by the falling dinosaur's massive body. Banjo got up and ran back towards Arbee, Sam and Lee.

The second Ceratosaur jumped in and grabbed one of

the small feather-covered meat eaters. It screamed as the Ceratosaur's teeth sunk into its body. Blood was splattering everywhere. The helpless animal was consumed in just two bites.

Then, the giant meat-eater grabbed one of the Birdosaurs that had been knocked out and made a quick meal of it.

It was a messy prehistoric food fight.

But then things got even crazier.

With all the screeching and squawking by all the Birdosaurs, and then the attack of the two Ceratosaurs, the Stegosaurus herd panicked and started to STAMPEDE!

"EVERYONE GET TO THE SHUTTLE CRAFT NOW!" screamed Arbee.

But Banjo would not leave without Dino. "DINO, DINOOOO!" he screamed. "DINO COME NOW!"

But, no matter how loud Banjo called, Dino did not come.

"We will find him from the air and pick him up," said Arbee. "We must leave now before we are either eaten or trampled to death!"

"DINO!" Banjo called again.

COME ... ON!" yelled Lee. "We'll find him later. Get in the shuttle Banjo!"

Sam ran over to Banjo and grabbed him by the arm. "We can't help Dino if we are dead!" she said in a calm but firm voice. "Let's go Banjo ... now please!"

Banjo, finally realizing that it was hopeless, ran with Sam back aboard the shuttle craft.

Arbee quickly flew the ship up to a safe height above the wild mess on the ground below.

There were small meat-eaters running everywhere and big meat-eaters trying to eat them. Then there were stampeding Stegosaurs wildly swinging their spiked tails in the air.

It was like a prehistoric war zone.

"We have got to find Dino, Arbee!" pleaded Banjo. "He will die down there!"

"We will," answered Arbee. "Tell me, does Dino still have his collar on, the one I gave him with the locater coin in it?"

Banjo held up Dino's empty collar and the attached leash. "No," he replied. "That crazy dog slipped out of it when we were attacked by the bird dinosaurs."

"Do not worry," Arbee assured him. "We will find him. Banjo, show me where Dino entered the forest."

"There," said Banjo, pointing to a spot to the right of the shuttle craft. "He ran after the rest of those Birdosaur things and chased them into the forest right there."

"All right," replied Arbee. "Samantha, would you use the computer sensors and start looking for life forms that are about Dino's size, please?"

"Yes," Sam answered. "I am searching now."

Arbee flew the shuttle over the part of the forest where

Dino disappeared.

"There is nothing close by here," said Sam.

They flew farther and farther into the woods when …

"Arbee, I have got something," said Sam. "It's not moving and it is just barely alive. It's to the left … in that clearing … over there."

"Dino?" gasped Banjo. "Oh no, please, don't be Dino!"

Chapter Two
DISAPPEARING DINO

Arbee flew the round shuttle craft between the tall redwood trees, down to a small grass and fern covered clearing.

"Whatever it is should be next to those bushes on the right, Arbee," said Sam as she looked at the computer screen.

"All right," replied Arbee, "we will go down and have a look."

Banjo held his breath as the ship floated closer to the spot where the mysterious body lay. "Please don't be Dino. Please don't be Dino," he whispered.

"I see it!" yelled Lee. "It's not Dino! It's not him!"

Banjo let out his breath with relief.

"It's one of those Birdosaur things, I think," added Lee.

There, lying in the red dirt among the grass and

ferns was one of the small feathered meat-eaters that had attacked the Science Team earlier.

It was dying from a wound on its neck. The wound was bleeding badly and the injured creature had only a short time to live.

Arbee brought the ship down as close as he could to look for clues. He did not dare land the shuttle and get outbecause there were still dangerous dinosaurs running around hunting for food.

"If I am not mistaken," said Arbee, "that is a dog bite on that dinosaur's back."

"Score one for Dino," said Banjo. "But where'd he go? He has got to be around here somewhere."

"There are dog paw prints around the dinosaur's body," mentioned Arbee.

"Yeah, and they are leading off in that direction," said Lee, "toward that muddy swamp. Dino must have been after something..."

"Or running away from something," interrupted Banjo, "like a Ceratosaur."

"Let us follow the trail," said Arbee. "I will fly as low as I possibly can. Everybody keep an eye on those dog tracks."

"Hey, Arbee," said Sam. "Did you notice that those small meat-eater dinosaurs have feathers on their bodies, kind of like birds?"

"I did," said Arbee. "When we recover Dino we must

study them more closely. I have not seen them before today."

"Lots of paleontologists think that birds are dinosaurs and considering all the dinosaurs we have seen with feathers on them, I think they are right," said Banjo, as he kept a close eye on Dino's trail. "Hey Arbee, Dino's tracks go over that way along the swamp and there are smaller meat-eater tracks, too."

"I think he is chasing another one of those bird things, a Birdosaur," added Lee.

"Yeah," replied Banjo. "I think Lee's right. The footprints are the right size."

"Man! Dino must have been really mad at those 'Birdosaurs'," said Sam.

"Dino is a very devoted dog," said Arbee. "He is very protective of his friends and especially his family. I only wish he would not run off like this. When we find him I must have a talk with him about that."

"Let's hope nothing ate him," said Banjo. "Sometimes his mouth is bigger than his mind."

"Do not underestimate him, Banjo," assured Arbee. "Dino is smarter than many people think. I have seen him get out of more dangerous situations than this. Do you remember how many times he escaped from that family of Tyrannosaurs we ran into a few months ago?'

"Yeah … I guess," Banjo sighed. "He is a lucky dog. I just hope his luck hasn't run out." Banjo was very worried.

They followed the trail for a while until they found

another one of the feathered dinosaurs. It was dead and partially eaten.

"Holy cows!" said Lee, "Do you think Dino ate that dinosaur?"

"I don't know. He is probably hungry," said Banjo. "Besides, he catches and eats squirrels around my house all the time. Those 'Birdosaurs' might seem like chickens to him."

"I guess," replied Lee. "I mean, they do have feathers and stuff. But maybe something else ate it."

They continued to follow Dino's tracks until the trail disappeared in the dark, thick forest. Arbee flew the ship everywhere and even got out of the shuttle to try to locate Dino's trail, but he could not find any dog prints.

He did find some large meat-eater tracks, which bothered him. He did not tell the others about the big footprints. He did not want to worry Banjo any more than he already had. There was no blood or dog hair anywhere, which was good news for Dino.

"Dino most likely escaped," Arbee thought. "These big footprints were probably made at another time."

Sam was frantically searching for life forms. "Nothing but big dinosaurs," she sighed. "No Dino-sized animals."

The sun was setting now and it was rapidly getting dark. Everyone was tired.

"I am going to fly back to our original position," said Arbee, "to the place where we were watching the Stegosaurs and where we were attacked."

"Yeah, good idea," said Banjo.

"That makes sense," said Lee. "If he was looking for us he would go back there, I think."

They quickly arrived at their original landing site but could not see Dino anywhere.

"Let me get out and call him," pleaded Banjo. "Maybe he is hiding somewhere, waiting for me."

Arbee landed the shuttle and they all got out.

"Samantha, Lee and I will stand guard while you call for Dino," Arbee told Banjo.

Banjo walked out to the place where he had last seen Dino, being careful to step around all the blood stains and body parts of the fierce Birdosaurs that had attacked them earlier.

"What a mess! There must have been a Ceratosaur feeding frenzy after we left, like a bunch of land sharks," said Lee, holding his sling shot loaded with a flash marble ready to shoot.

"All right Banjo, we are ready. Try calling Dino," said Arbee.

"DINO!" yelled Banjo as loud as he could. "DINO COME HERE ... DINO ... HERE BOY!"

Banjo called for almost a half hour straight, but still nothing. There was no Dino.

Sam, Lee and Arbee called also. Arbee, whose

electronic body floated off the ground, looked all around but found no sign of the missing Chow Chow dog.

A full moon was rising above a distant mountain range, lighting up the whole valley. The Science Team could see the large herd of Stegosaurs they had seen earlier, far out in a fern-covered plain. They were crowding together and settling in for the night.

The adult Stegosaurs were around the outside with their deadly tails aimed outward, forming a sort of spiked fort. The younger animals, including the babies, were standing in the middle of the herd for protection from predators.

No Allosaur or its smaller cousin, Ceratosaur, would dare attack a fortress of Stegosaurus spikes and plates.

Banjo, Lee and Sam were still calling for Dino when Arbee interrupted them. "We need to take a break and you need to eat something," he told them. "None of you have eaten since breakfast."

"I am not hungry," complained Banjo. "I want to look for my dog."

"Well, I am starved," said Lee. "I could eat a whole cow."

"Banjo, I will make an agreement with you. Let me make you something to eat. Then we will come back to this spot in the shuttle and we will camp out here until we find Dino," said Arbee. "How does that sound?"

"Okay," he replied at last, "but I am still not very hungry."

"Come on Banjo," said Sam. "If we are going to stay up all night and look for Dino then we all need food."

They were walking slowly back to the shuttle craft nearby when Banjo heard something rustling in the bushes. "Wait, I hear something ... Dino ... is that you, DINO?" he called out.

Arbee and the team waited anxiously. The rustling noise got louder.

"DINO, COME!" yelled Banjo. He took out and loaded his sling shot. He was not going to take any chances.

Suddenly something ran from the tree line, moving towards the team quickly and quietly. It was definitely NOT a dog, but a large meat-eating dinosaur.

THWACK – Banjo shot first.

THWACK, THWACK – Sam and Lee fired.

FLASH, FLASH, FLASH – The beast was a young Allosaur. It dropped down like a bag of potatoes – BOOSCH – into the bushes.

"Eat that you lousy, stinking dinosaur!" yelled an angry Banjo.

The team quickly climbed aboard the shuttle craft. Arbee flew the ship off into the night with no Dino on board, and absolutely no idea where the dog was or if he was even still alive.

What was worse, they had no idea where to start looking for him.

A tear slowly rolled down Banjo's cheek as he stared out of the ship and across the moonlit forest and plains.

Chapter Three
THE SEARCH

Within a few minutes the shuttle craft had arrived back at the starship.

Sam, who was standing next to Arbee, pushed some buttons on the computer control board, opening a hatch leading to the big starship's top deck. That was deck number five, where the shuttle dock and the bridge were.

The large round silver starship was camouflaged with electronic screens, which made it look like part of the forest around it. This was so dinosaurs would not be scared away.

Arbee carefully parked the shuttle. Then he and the Science Team walked to the bridge, which was on the opposite side of the same deck as the shuttle dock.

They found Zinzu working away putting data into some computers with his eight arms and eight eyes working rapidly on three different computers.

"Must be nice to have a robot body that can float and never needs sleep," said Sam.

"Yeah," agreed Lee. "But if I had one of those robot bodies, mine would look like a super hero with big muscles."

"Why?" asked Sam. "You don't need big muscles if you are a robot and you can float."

Lee thought for a moment, "Because … it would look … awesome, that's why."

"Whatever!" laughed Sam, shaking her head.

Banjo was very quiet, not his usual joking self. He was too worried about Dino.

Arbee updated Zinzu on what had happened to their friend Dino and how the search for him had failed to turn up anything.

Zinzu thought for a minute. "You know," he said finally, "in my spare time I have been working on improving one of the ship's computer sensors so that it will not only locate a single life form but also who or what the life form is."

"So, you mean you could find out exactly where Dino is?" asked Banjo.

"Yes, if I programmed all the data about Dino into the computer," said Zinzu, "we could find out where he is without having to look at every living creature that is his size."

"How long before you can finish with the new sensor?" asked Arbee.

"I would say eight hours, possibly less," replied Zinzu.

"But we don't have eight hours," Banjo protested. "Dino will never last that long."

"What if I helped you?" asked Sam. "Would that speed things up?"

"Yes. Yes it would," he replied. "We could have it ready to go in three or four hours, I believe."

"All right, Zinzu, go ahead and start on this but I want you to try to get this done in three hours instead of four," said Arbee.

"I will work for completion in three hours then," said Zinzu. "I will start at once. Samantha, I will see you when you have finished eating. Right?" said Zinzu.

"Yes, right!" she replied. "I'll be quick."

"Good. You and I have much work to do," said Zinzu. He flew to the far side of the bridge and went to work on the new computer sensor.

"How about I make you all something fast?" asked Arbee. "Would hamburgers do?"

They all agreed. Arbee made them cheeseburgers and something to drink. Sam quickly finished hers and excused herself to help Zinzu.

"Don't worry, Banjo," she said, patting him on his shoulder. "We'll find him."

She walked over to Bootsey, her cat, who had just finished eating and she scratched him behind the ears. "We lost Dino, Boots, and we are trying to get him back," she said. Then she ran off to help Zinzu build the new sensor.

"You mean HE lost you," thought Bootsey. "Typical dog, always following their noses and not paying any attention to where they are going. It looks like he needs my help ... AGAIN!"

Bootsey went over to Arbee and pawed at him. He wanted to make a suggestion to the alien on how to find Dino.

One of Arbee's skills was his ability to speak with animals through his mind.

Arbee turned to Bootsey. "Yes, Bootsey, what can I do for you? Do you want more food?"

"No, I don't need more food," thought Bootsey. "Take me with you when you search for Dino. Not only can I sense signs and tracks you can't, especially with my nose, but if I get close enough I will be able to hear his thoughts even better than you."

"Thank you for your offer," replied Arbee, "but you must promise not to run away. I cannot lose two Science Team members in one day. Samantha would never forgive me."

"Cats don't run away unless their owners are mean or they are being chased by something. Anyway, I didn't run away from you when we were studying those flying giant bird things. You guys left ME behind and I had to find YOU, remember?" thought Bootsey. "Just take me with you."

"I see what you are saying. All right," said Arbee. "I can use all the help I can get."

Lee and Banjo finished their food and came over to Arbee. Banjo looked a little better.

"Can we go back out and look for Dino now Arbee?" he asked.

"Yes, of course," Arbee replied. "Bring some blankets and I will bring some food. You can both take turns looking for Dino. Oh, and Bootsey is coming along as well. He says he can help us find Dino."

"Any help we can get is fine with me," said Banjo. "Just don't run off, cat. We have enough problems."

"Relax kid," thought Bootsey. "Do you want me to find that silly dog of yours or not? Besides, cats are not a problem, people are."

The boys grabbed their gear and met Arbee at the shuttle craft. They climbed aboard, followed by Bootsey.

Arbee took off, flying the shuttle out of the starship and into the moonlit prehistoric night.

The moon seemed bigger in this time than in the present and the stars were so bright that they looked like millions of glowing diamonds on a dark blue cloth.

Arbee made a call over the shuttle's radio, "Arbee to Zinzu, come in please."

"Zinzu here, go ahead,"

"We will be landing at the location where Dino disappeared in case he returns. Let me know the minute you have that new sensor working," said Arbee.

"Will do, Zinzu out."

After a short flight, Arbee landed the shuttle craft

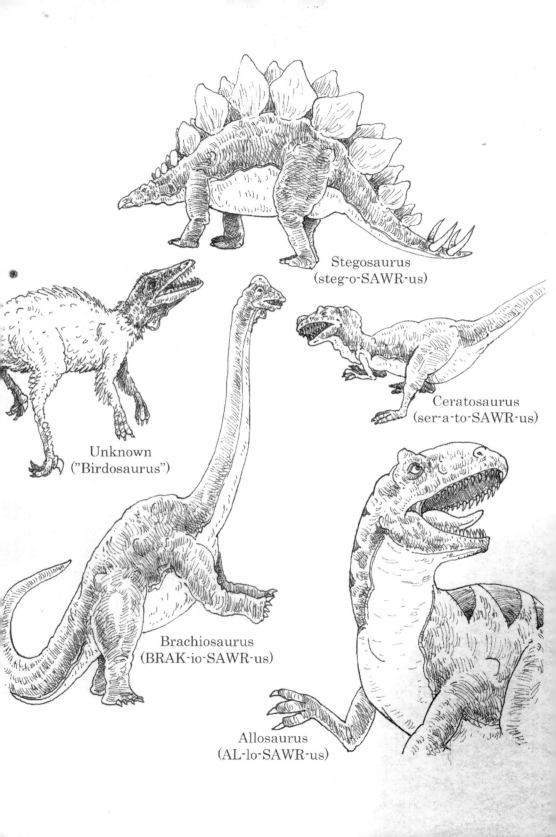

Stegosaurus
(steg-o-SAWR-us)

Unknown
("Birdosaurus")

Ceratosaurus
(ser-a-to-SAWR-us)

Brachiosaurus
(BRAK-io-SAWR-us)

Allosaurus
(AL-lo-SAWR-us)

near the spot where they had last seen Dino. The boys got out their sling shots and loaded them.

Arbee opened the door and turned on some lights around the outside of the shuttle so they could see clearly. Also, if Dino was around he would see the lights and find his way back to the craft.

"Stay alert, you two," cautioned Arbee. "I will be right behind keeping an eye on things."

"Okay," said Lee. "Hey, Banjo, wait up!"

Banjo was already out the door calling for his lost dog. "DINO, DINO COME, COME ON BOY. COME HERE DINO!" Banjo called to Dino for the next half hour.

This was starting to make Lee very nervous. "I can't believe that we haven't been attacked by every Allosaur within twenty miles," he whispered.

"Tough beans, I don't care. Let them attack," growled Banjo. "I'll blast those overgrown parrots." He was concentrating on one thing – finding Dino!

While Banjo and Lee were looking for Dino, Bootsey had been sniffing the ground. All the bits and pieces of the feathered dinosaurs had been picked up by other scavenging animals.

The blood stains on the ground were the only things that were left from the attack. They were being eaten up quickly by insects. Nothing went to waste in this world.

"Well, Bootsey," said Arbee, "anything to report?"

"Yes," thought Bootsey. "I smell Dino, but the scent

is old and so are his tracks. I have been all through these bushes and I tell you, Dino is not here and has not been here for a long time. I do not smell him in the air currents, so we need to look somewhere else."

"I see," said Arbee. "That is most discouraging."

"Yes I know. What we should do is to try and pick up his trail where you lost it," thought Bootsey. "That is our only chance."

"Very well," thought Arbee. "Thank you for your help."

"Thank me when we find him," thought Bootsey. "Let's hurry. Dino being lost out here is like a mouse in a room full of cats. He is a smart dog but he can't hide out forever in this place."

"Right you are," said Arbee, as he picked up Bootsey and hurried back to the ship.

"Banjo, Lee, you need to get on board the shuttle," commanded Arbee. "Bootsey has been sniffing around and Dino is not here and has not been here since he left. We are going to try to pick up his trail where we lost it."

The boys ran aboard the shuttle without argument, followed by Arbee and the cat.

Bootsey looked over at the herd of Stegosaurs camped out for the night and for just a split second thought, "That smell ... could it be? It's coming from that bunch of big cow-lizards with the plates on their backs and spikes on their tails." Bootsey smelled again, but he had lost the scent.

"Bootsey, we need to leave," said Arbee. "Did you smell

something?"

"I am not sure," Bootsey replied. "I thought for a second I smelled Dino, but it's gone now. Take me back to where you lost the trail ... now!"

Chapter Four
DETECTIVE BOOTSEY

Back on the starship Zinzu and Samantha were busily working nonstop to get the new sensor working.

Sam was helping as best she could, but the computer sensor they were working on was very advanced alien science and a lot more complicated than any computer she had ever seen.

She had a hard time understanding it, even after everything Arbee had taught her.

"This is pretty complicated stuff," she sighed.

"Do not feel bad," replied Zinzu. "This is difficult even for me, and this is my job! Would you please hand me the connecting tool? It is the blue one to your left."

"Okay ... here," she replied and handed him a strange, fork-looking instrument which he used to connect some wires.

"Thank you," he answered. "All right ... there ... that

should … do it. Let us give it a try. Samantha, I need you to type in everything you know about Dino. I need his height, weight, everything."

"Okay," said Sam. "I have a card that Banjo gave me. It has all the data about Dino on it. I'll type it in. Let's see, the type of body is Canine. The type of dog is a Chow Chow and his weight is seventy eight pounds …"

Sam typed in everything on Banjo's card plus anything else she or Zinzu could remember. She even put in a photograph of Dino that Banjo had.

"Done," she said at last. "That's everything that I have."

"Good," replied Zinzu. "Arbee had some data on Dino in his files, too. I am entering that now."

"Okay, now what?" asked Sam.

"Now we push this button here and hope it works," answered Zinzu. "It should locate Dino if he is within twenty miles of the ship." Zinzu pushed the button and he and Sam waited, anxiously watching the computer sensor screen.

Outside it was now dawn, the nighttime sky and stars were slowly fading away as the sun rose.

Since they had no luck finding any trace of Dino at the place where they were attacked, Arbee ordered everyone back on board the shuttle craft. They flew to the last place where they had seen any trace of the missing dog.

After landing, Arbee, Bootsey and Banjo left the ship to continue their search. Lee, who was exhausted from searching all night, was sound asleep on the floor of the shuttle.

"Just leave him," said Banjo. "Lee could sleep through a war."

They went to where Dino's tracks disappeared into a thick clump of bushes that were growing into a large swamp. "Put me down here, Arbee," Bootsey thought.

The cat started looking around using his 'super cat senses,' as he called them.

Arbee floated behind Bootsey, while Banjo stood guard with his sling shot loaded. They worked their way through the bushes and moved along the shore of the shallow swamp.

Off in the distance they heard a loud animal call, like the sound of deep-voiced elephants. Banjo looked up. "Arbee," he whispered, "look across the swamp. Look at the size of those things!"

Arbee stopped and saw a herd of huge beasts moving through the forest eating the leaves on the highest branches of the trees. They had gray-brown skin, massive bodies and legs, and long necks that made them taller than any tree in the forest.

"They look like Brachiosaurs to me," said Banjo.

"Yes," replied Arbee. "Brachiosaurs is the name your paleontologists have given them. They are one of the largest land animals to have ever existed on this planet."

"They are the biggest dinosaurs we have seen on any of our trips," whispered Banjo.

"Yeoww," said Bootsey. "Just make sure one of those things doesn't step on me," he thought. "Now let's get back to work. Arbee, come look over here."

Arbee floated over. "I see, Bootsey. Those are Dino's tracks," he said, "You have found his trail again. Excellent."

"Dino was walking in the water. There is a faint dog print underwater, in the mud," thought Bootsey. "It's an old animal trick to make sure you're not being followed. Water messes up your scent trail so it's hard for things to follow you. Cats invented it. Humans said they invented it, but they lie. It was cats. I think one of those big bird-lizard things was chasing him."

Bootsey continued to scamper along the shoreline of the swamp, being careful not to get his feet wet. Many cats, like Bootsey, hate getting their feet wet. "Dino went this way, along the swamp. I can smell him, but just barely."

"What's going on?" asked Banjo. "Has he found something?"

"Bootsey has picked up Dino's scent," said Arbee. "Bootsey, wait. We should go back to the ship and bring it closer to the trail. We are getting too far away from it."

Bootsey agreed. "I think this trail goes on for a while," he thought. "Here, catch!" Bootsey leaped into Arbee's arms. "It's faster if you carry me, plus I don't want to get my feet muddy and mess up the carpet in your flying thingy. We cats like to stay clean, you know."

Banjo, Arbee and Bootsey made their way back to the shuttle. They were nearly there when Banjo stopped ... "Hold up," he whispered. "We've got visitors!"

Arbee stopped. "Oh, blast! I should have put the shuttle's camouflage screen on."

Standing over the shuttle were two Allosaurs. They were curiously, but very quietly, looking over the shuttle craft trying to figure out what it was and if they could eat it.

One was sniffing it, while the other lightly tapped the glass top with a claw on one of its fingers.

Banjo thought that they looked funny, like confused chickens. "Man, these things are PESTS!" he complained. "Let me shoot them." He raised his sling shot and was about to fire at the first Allosaur when Arbee stopped him.

"Banjo, let me deal with this. But stay alert in case there are other Allosaurs in the woods ready to attack us," said Arbee. "Remember what happened when we were in this time period before."

Arbee was talking about the time they were trying to get a baby long-necked plant-eater back to its herd. The Science Team was attacked by nearly a dozen Allosaurs.

"I'll be ready," replied Banjo. "I know these things like to hang out in packs."

Arbee flew off to meet the curious meat-eaters. As he got closer, the two dinosaurs turned their attention to him. The moment the Allosaurs saw Arbee, he pushed a button on his chest and burst into flame.

"Awesome," said Banjo. He had seen Arbee do this trick before to scare off a Tyrannosaurus Rex.

The burning alien flew directly at the pair of surprised Allosaurs. This caused them to jump back. Arbee moved even closer, forcing the Allosaurs to run back into the forest.

Arbee had discovered that dinosaurs had a fear of fire.

Arbee turned off the fake flames that covered his body and became his normal self again.

He was about to float back to the ship when he heard a loud roar behind him. He turned to see another, even larger Allosaur charging him from a different part of the forest.

FLASH – The dinosaur never made it out of the bushes before Banjo shot him with his sling shot.

"Sleep tight, bird-brain!" grumbled Banjo. "Hey, Arbee, let's get out of here before this place turns into camp Allosaur." Banjo grabbed Bootsey and ran towards the shuttle craft.

"I agree," said Arbee.

Banjo, Bootsey and Arbee got aboard the shuttle, slammed the door shut and took off to pick up Dino's trail again. Lee Wong was still sleeping peacefully on the floor of the shuttle, as if nothing had happened.

"I cannot believe that Lee slept through all of that!" laughed Arbee.

"Told you he could sleep through a war," said Banjo, who smiled for the first time in two days.

Back at the starship, Zinzu and Sam were testing the new sensor.

Zinzu pushed the button on the computer control board and — ZZZZZZAP — the control board erupted in a shower of sparks that shot everywhere.

Zinzu quickly shut it off, stopping the spraying sparks. "Blast it!" he exclaimed. "I must have crossed a wire somewhere. Are you all right, Samantha?"

"Yeah," she sighed, as she shook the ashes out of her brown hair. "Well that didn't work, so now what do we do?"

Chapter Five
DINO IS HIDING ... WHERE?

"HERE!" thought Bootsey. "Dino was here in this mud puddle next to the swamp."

"Excellent!" said Arbee. "I do not know how I missed his trail."

"First, you are not a cat. And second, it is easy to do," thought Bootsey. "His tracks are almost completely covered with lots of these other tracks."

"What's going on?" asked Banjo.

"We are in luck. Bootsey has located Dino's trail again," answered Arbee. "He was here."

Banjo's hopes grew. "Good, then he has got to be **alive**," he said.

Bootsey's pace quickened as the trail got **easier for** the cat to follow. "See all these tracks? It's those **bird-lizard** things again," he thought.

"Allosaurs," corrected Arbee.

"Yeah, whatever," thought Bootsey. "I think Dino was running away and was looking for a hiding place from those … Allo… those bird-lizard things."

They moved further along until the search party finally arrived outside of the forest, at the edge of a large fern-covered plain. Arbee looked off into the distance at the big herd of Stegosaurs grazing nearly two miles away.

He could hear them calling to one another with grunts and mooing sounds.

"He went that way," thought Bootsey. "THAT was his PLAN. Do you see? I think Dino is hiding with that bunch of spiky tail cow-lizards. Hmmm, there is some other weird smell here along with Dino's, but I don't know what it is … never mind."

"Well Banjo, if Bootsey is right – and I believe he is – Dino is hiding somewhere in that herd of Stegosaurs," said Arbee, pointing to the herd on the distant plain.

"Great! So what are we waiting for?" said Banjo. "Let's go find him and get him out of there."

"Back to the shuttle at once!" commanded Arbee. "We do not have a moment to lose!"

"No kidding," thought Bootsey. "That is NOT a good place to hide, silly dog … what was he thinking?"

The bridge of the starship was a mess. Bits of burnt wire, metal and computer circuit boards were laying everywhere. Sam was busy replacing a green and blue cable in the back of one of the sensor computers, while Zinzu was putting new circuit boards into another one.

Zinzu had discovered what had caused the sensor computer to explode. He had incorrectly switched two of the circuit boards and it had taken a long time to figure out what had happened.

"Okay, the main cables are connected," said Sam, as she tried to wipe the black ash off her face.

"That is good," replied Zinzu. "It should be ready now. Stand back, Samantha, in case it explodes again."

Sam did not need to be warned. She was already standing behind another computer station for protection. "Okay, Zinzu, go ahead, try it again," she said as she covered her eyes.

Zinzu double checked that all the data about Dino had been entered into the computer's memory and pushed the button for the second time.

"Come on computer," whispered Sam, "WORK."

Lee Wong had finally awakened from his long nap and was trying to straighten out his messed up black hair. He stumbled over to look out the shuttle's glass top. "Anything happening?" he asked. "Any sign of Dino?"

"Yeah, a lot happened. First of all ... you slept through an Allosaur attack at our last stop," laughed Banjo.

"No way. I did not. You are such a liar," Lee replied.

"I swear!" insisted Banjo. "They were looking in the top of the shuttle right at you! I can't believe you didn't hear them. They were trying to figure out how to eat you."

"Arbee, is he telling the truth?" asked Lee, doubtfully.

"I am afraid so," replied Arbee, who was busy flying the shuttle craft towards the big herd of Stegosaurs.

"This place is so dangerous I can't believe it," mumbled Lee. "I am glad these psycho dinosaurs are extinct. They are always attacking and eating stuff. If my mom EVER knew what I was doing … she … would … freak … out. Hey, speaking of food, do we have anything to eat?" he added. "I am starving."

Banjo dug into one of his pockets and pulled out one of Arbee's food computer granola bars. "Here … catch!" he said, as he tossed the bar to Lee.

"Cool. Thanks," said Lee. "So, any luck finding Dino?"

"Bootsey believes that Dino is hiding inside that herd of Stegosaurs," answered Arbee. "We are continuing our search there and …" Arbee was interrupted by an urgent call from the starship.

"Zinzu to Arbee, come in Arbee."

"Arbee here, go ahead Zinzu," Arbee replied.

"I have good news to report. The new locator sensor is working," said Zinzu.

"Excellent!" replied Arbee. "Do you have a location on Dino yet?"

"Yes, we do," replied Zinzu. "Dino is located right in

the middle of a large herd of dinosaurs."

"Stegosaurs," interrupted Sam. "Dino is in the middle of the Stegosaurus herd. He is with all the babies in the middle."

"Yes, but … is he alive?" asked Arbee.

"Oh yes, he is very much alive," replied Zinzu.

"Good news," Arbee said, "very good news and excellent work, you two. We will take it from here. By the way, what took so long?"

"That's a long story," said Sam. "We kind of had an accident and messed up the bridge, a little."

"There was no major damage, I hope," said Arbee.

"Some computer wires and circuit boards burned up in an earlier test," said Zinzu. "But the damage is not major.

"Zinzu and I have some serious cleaning up to do," added Sam

"All right, we will be back as soon as we have rescued Dino … Arbee out."

"HAH! What did I tell you?" thought Bootsey. "Wasn't I right? I was right! Dino IS in the herd of spiky tail cow-lizards … Sensors … CATS don't need no stinking sensors!"

"You were right, Bootsey," laughed Arbee. "Boys, we should thank our cat friend here for his help. He was the one who pointed us in the right direction."

Lee applauded the proud cat. Bootsey was purring and happily cleaning himself.

"Thanks, Bootsey," said Banjo and he gave Bootsey a hug.

"Easy kid, don't mess up the fur," thought Bootsey.

"All right Banjo, we know Dino is alive and he is somewhere in the middle of that herd of Stegosaurs," said Arbee. "But when we rescue him, we do not want to make any sudden movements or noises which might cause them to stampede and harm Dino."

"Okay, so why don't we just find him first," said Banjo, "then we can figure out how to get him out of there."

"Agreed," answered Arbee. "First, I will camouflage the ship so we do not scare the Stegosaurs." Arbee pushed some buttons on the shuttle craft's control board, making the small round ship disappear. Then he flew over the middle of the herd to start the search.

Arbee made a quick call to the starship, "This is Arbee to Zinzu, come in."

"Zinzu here, go ahead."

"Can you give me a more exact location for Dino?" asked Arbee. "The center of this herd is a rather large area."

There was a pause. "Dino is located in almost the exact middle of the herd with the babies. I am sending a computer image now," said Zinzu.

"I have the pictures now. Thank you. Arbee out. Banjo, Lee and Bootsey start looking for Dino," said Arbee. "I will fly as low as I can. Let me know when you have spotted him."

The boys each went to different sides of the shuttle to try to spot Dino. Bootsey jumped up on the control board so he could see, also.

The sun had gone down and it was getting dark fast, making it hard to see. Luckily, the moon was rising early which might give them some light.

Arbee floated the shuttle over the location that Zinzu had given him.

Arbee used the computer sensor to find animals which were about the same size as Dino, but there was a problem.

"There are so many baby Stegosaurs that are the same size as Dino. This will not be easy," mumbled Arbee. "Lee, there is an animal on your side that is about the right size. Can you see it?"

Lee stared at it for a moment. "Yeah, but it's a Stegosaur that is about the same size as Dino."

The search went on for about fifteen minutes. They must have looked at twenty different dinosaurs, then ...

"Wait a minute!" said Banjo. "I see something but it's weird ... it's covered with clumps of leaves or something. I don't think it's a Stegosaur."

Arbee stopped the shuttle, picked up Bootsey and, along with Lee, went to take a look.

"I think Banjo may be right. It doesn't look like any Stegosaur I have ever seen," said Lee.

Bootsey looked at the strange animal. "Arbee, it's him!" thought Bootsey. "It's Dino! I heard a thought from him! We have got to get him out of there now!"

"Bootsey says it is him," said Arbee. "Let me try to communicate with him. Hopefully we are close enough." He tried to send a thought to Dino.

The strange-looking animal looked up and thought, "Arbee, ARBEE ... IS THAT YOU?" Dino jumped up and barked, "Arf, arf, arf!"

Dino's bark was so loud that the baby Stegosaurs started getting restless and crying out. The older dinosaurs were also getting nervous.

Dino was about start a ... Stegosaurus STAMPEDE!

Chapter Six
RESCUE FOR ... TWO?

"Dino, stop barking!" thought Arbee.

"Yeah … shut … up … dog!" thought Bootsey. "We know where you are. Relax! We are here to save you. You are just making things worse."

"Okay, okay," thought Dino. "Sorry, but I thought you guys would never find me. Where are you?"

"We are right above you," thought Arbee. "Keep very still."

"We are in one of Arbee's invisible flying things," thought Bootsey, "the shuttle thing."

Dino stopped barking and jumping up and down. It took a few minutes, but the baby Stegosaurs finally calmed down and one by one went back to sleep.

"I can't believe we found him!" exclaimed Banjo.

"Finally!" said Lee. "Let's use the lift-beams, pick him up or whatever and get the heck out of here so we can go eat. I am starving and I have got to go to the bathroom."

"So how do we get him out?" asked Banjo, "Can we pick him up with the shuttle's lift-beam and carry him to a safe place?"

"The lifter beam is too bright," replied Arbee. "It might make the herd panic and Dino could get trampled."

"Dude, just tell him to sneak out through the sleeping Stegos," said Lee impatiently. "Then when he is safely out in the open, we will pick him up, easy peasy."

"Let me tell the plan to Dino," said Arbee.

"No, I'll tell him," thought Bootsey. "Dino, walk through the herd and into the clearing and we will pick you up. I don't know why you didn't do that earlier."

"I CAN'T!" thought Dino. "That is the problem. These stupid cow-lizards think I am one of their babies. Every time I try to get out of the herd the big spiky tail cow-lizard block my way. That's why I didn't go back to the first place we were at."

"I … am … TRAPPED! Besides, there is another dog here," thought Dino. "He is my friend. He saved me and I can't leave him because he needs my help!"

"What?" thought Bootsey. "Another dog? That must have been that other weird scent I smelled earlier."

"Another DOG?" exclaimed Arbee.

"What? What's the matter?" asked Banjo, alarmed.

"Dino says there is another DOG with him," said Arbee. "But that is not possible, not in this time."

"Everyone knows dogs haven't been invented yet," yawned Lee. "It must be some kind of weird dinosaur."

"Dino, are you positive," thought Arbee, "a dog? There are no dogs in this time."

"I … am … positive," thought Dino. "He is a dog. He is right here beside me. I think he is from another planet or something, so you have to save us both."

"Alright, hold for a moment," thought Arbee to Dino.

"Well, now we have two dogs that need rescuing. If anyone has any good ideas how we could accomplish this without causing the Stegosaurs to stampede, now would be a good time to share it," said Arbee, who seemed impatient.

Banjo thought for a moment. "How about if you lowered one of us by a rope and we grab the dogs and you pull us up. No wait, that won't work. Maybe we should go ahead and risk using the lift-beam but make the pick up really fast, before the Stegos freak out."

"Hold on, hold on, why don't we just land," suggested Lee, "and do it real slow so we gently push the baby Stegos out of the way? Then we open the hatch, grab the dogs and blast out of here."

"Hmmm," said Arbee. He floated over to the shuttle's control board and pushed some buttons. "Bootsey, just ahead of us there is a spot where there are very few babies. Tell Dino and his friend to go there and quietly nudge the baby Stegosaurs outward to make the clearing bigger," thought Arbee, "and have him do it now, please."

Bootsey told Dino the plan then Dino and his friend

sneaked to the small clearing and, using their heads, very gently and very slowly began pushing the babies out of the way without waking them up.

"What are you going to do?" asked Banjo.

"I am going to follow Lee's suggestion and land the shuttle. Hopefully, without bothering the baby dinosaurs," replied Arbee.

"Yeah, you see? That is MY plan!" Lee said proudly.

"Yeah, well don't be looking for your trophy just yet super-star," warned Banjo, "until we have the dogs on board and we are out of here."

"Oh, it will work, trust me," said Lee.

"Banjo, you and Lee must be ready to push the button that opens the shuttle's hatch," said Arbee. "Then, help the dogs get aboard as quickly as possible. Bootsey, tell the dogs to go to the edge of the clearing and wait. Tell them to be ready to jump into the shuttle the instant the hatch is open."

"Dino," thought Bootsey, "you dogs go to the edge of the clearing and stay there. We are coming down. Be ready to jump in when you see the door open."

"Okay," thought Dino. Both dogs moved to the edge of the clearing and waited.

"Ready," thought Bootsey to Arbee.

"We are all set," said Banjo, who had his hand on the 'Hatch Open' button. Lee was on the opposite side, ready to grab the dogs and pull them in, if necessary.

"Right. Here we go," said Arbee. He slowly lowered the still invisible shuttle craft toward the ground. Lower and lower it went. One of the baby Stegosaurs started to wander into the clearing but was gently shoved aside by the descending ship.

"Phew!" whispered Lee. "We didn't wake him up. So far, we are good."

The ship continued moving downward until finally, after what seemed like the longest time, the shuttle craft touched down softly – f o o f.

"We have landed," whispered Arbee. "I am dimming the inside lights. Bootsey, tell the dogs it is time."

"Okay, Dino, pay attention and watch for the hatch," thought Bootsey. "And don't mess this up. We have one chance to do this."

"We are ready," thought Dino.

"Banjo, push the button ... NOW!" said Arbee.

WHAP – Banjo hit the button and – SWISH – the hatch flew open. A loud sound filled the ship. The sleeping Stegosaurs were snoring.

"Dino, here," Banjo called, loud enough to be heard over the snorts, grunts and whistles of the sleeping Stegosaurs.

Dino and the other dog wasted no time. They ran and leaped into the shuttle.

Banjo was about to close the hatch when a sleepy-eyed baby Stegosaurus stuck its head into the opening. Lee thought fast and tried to quietly shoo the dinosaur back outside by pushing its head. "Get out of here ... go, go, go on," said Lee.

"Wraaa!" it cried out in protest.

"Shhh, shhh, it's okay, little guy, looky here," said Lee as he reached into his pocket and pulled out his half-eaten granola bar. He held it up to the baby Stegosaur's mouth. "Eat this, it's good. See? Yummy ... gra ... no ... la ... bar."

The baby Stegosaur first sniffed it then grabbed the food and started chomping on it. "Raaumf!" it mumbled. It spit out the granola bar and walked back into the darkness.

"Now, Banjo!" said Lee. "Close the hatch."

Banjo hit the button and – WHOOSH – the hatch slammed shut.

"Okay, Arbee," said Banjo. "We have got them. Let's go!"

Banjo hugged Dino, even though Dino was covered with dirt and leaves from head to toe. He was so relieved to see him. "Dino ... you're safe," he whispered.

"Boy am I glad to see you," thought Dino.

"Good job," said Arbee. He flew the ship up slowly until he was high above the still sleeping herd, then took off like a bullet back to the starship.

Arbee made a call to the starship, "Arbee to Zinzu, come in."

"Zinzu here," he replied.

"We have two dogs in need of cleaning and possible

body repair," said Arbee.

"Please repeat … did you say TWO dogs?" asked Zinzu, sounding confused.

"That is correct … two dogs," repeated Arbee.

"I see … well … Samantha and I will prepare everything. Zinzu, out."

When the shuttle craft finally landed aboard the starship, Sam and Zinzu were there to greet everyone.

"Oh my gosh," gasped Sam. "Dino, you are a mess! You're covered with leaves and mud, you poor thing. So this must be your new friend. He is a cute little guy!"

Sam scratched the mystery dog behind his ears, which made him wag his tail.

The strange-looking dog was smaller than Dino. His long hair was a dark reddish brown with some black spots. He had a wolf-like head with a body that looked like it belonged to a baby bear. On his behind was a big, bushy tail. He had thick legs and big paws. He did not look like any dog anyone had ever seen anywhere before.

Banjo thought he looked like he was put together from a bunch of different animals. "He is like a bear wolf...or something."

"Everyone to the Light Shower," ordered Zinzu. "You are all a mess and are tracking dirt on my nice, clean starship. You too Sam, so you can clean all the black ash off of your face, hair and arms."

As they went to get cleaned up Dino turned to Arbee

and thought, "I am sorry I caused so much trouble. Thanks for saving me. I didn't do it on purpose, you know."

"You are welcome, my friend," thought Arbee. "We will talk about this later. I want to hear the whole story, especially the part about the Stegosaurs. After all, you lived with them for nearly three days!"

"Yeah, without any sleep!" thought Dino. "Did you hear how loud those things snore? It was the worst."

Zinzu led everyone to Light Shower. "Everyone on the platform, please," he said.

After being covered in different colored lights, they were cleaned up in just a few minutes. The Light Shower cleaned their clothes, hair, faces, everything, without using a drop of water.

They felt much better, especially Dino, who must have been covered with at least five pounds of dried mud and leaves.

"I am going to fix food for everyone before we do anything else," said Arbee.

Arbee prepared hot meals for Lee, Banjo and Sam as well as Bootsey, Dino and Dino's new dog friend. No one spoke a word until they had finished every scrap of food on their plates and in their bowls.

After the meal, Arbee turned to Dino and the mysterious dog. He said to Zinzu, "As I speak to the dogs here, will you translate what is said to the rest of the Science Team for me? I want to ask them some questions, but I must do it mentally."

"Certainly," replied Zinzu.

Like Arbee, Zinzu could speak to other life forms using thought.

Actually, the people of the planet Izikzah could hear the thoughts of any living thing and they could send thoughts to them, also.

It was a very good ability to have because they could talk to different life forms but did not have to know thousands of different languages. This skill was also helpful to them as librarians.

Everyone listened closely as Arbee floated down in front of the strange-looking dog and thought, "Hello, my name is Arbee. I am the captain of the starship you are aboard. We are time travelers from another planet. We are librarians on a peaceful research mission and we will not harm you in any way. You are safe with us. Do you understand?"

The dog looked over at Dino. He appeared to be afraid. "How do you know these people are not space pirates, Dino?" he thought.

Dino looked at him and thought, "Don't worry. You really ARE safe. Arbee will help you, I promise. He has helped me lots of times and they are definitely NOT space pirates."

The dog slowly walked over to Arbee, sat down, and raised his paw as a form of greeting. "My name is Teeg," he thought. "I am from this time but I am not from this world."

"I was separated from my owner whose space ship

is nearby. We were attacked by a pack of diamond-backed toothies," thought Teeg. "Dino calls them 'bird-lizards'.

"I need to get back to my ship. If my owner takes off and leaves me here I will not survive long. And I do not want to spend the rest of my life running away from the diamond-backed toothies. Can you help me ... Please?" he thought.

Chapter Seven
TOO MANY ALIENS

Arbee was trying to find out more about Teeg, the mysterious alien dog that they had rescued with Dino. "Teeg, can you tell me who your owner is and why you are on this planet?"

"Well, my owner's name is Captain Cliven Greck. He is an explorer for the empire," thought Teeg.

"An explorer for the empire?" asked Arbee.

"Yes, the empire ... you know, it is a big group of worlds that are part of a big civilization. My owner finds and explores new worlds to see if they have enough natural resources like air, water, minerals, plants and animals, you know, things like that," thought Teeg.

"The empire has a huge population and it is always looking for new worlds to inhabit. That is why we have been exploring this one," thought Teeg. "It is a nice place, but these toothies are just too dangerous. I do not think a colony would last very long here!"

"Tell me about it!" whispered Lee when he heard Zinzu's translation.

"Captain Greck thinks that this world might be a good colony if the Department of New Colonies, back in our home world, could figure out a way to control the animals," thought Teeg. "Anyway, about three days ago Captain Greck and I were attacked by a pack of the diamond-back toothy things. I was able to trick them into chasing me away from the Captain and our starship."

"That's one of my jobs ... to protect the ship," thought Teeg. "And I am very good at it, too. The toothies followed me into the woods where I lost them. As I was running away, I met Dino. I could not believe I found another dog. He was a mess and he needed help. We ran around in the forest hiding from the toothies until we saw the herd of spiky tailed things." Teeg could not think of how to describe the dinosaurs.

"Stegosaurs," thought Arbee. "We call them Stegos for short."

"I call them cow-lizards," thought Dino. "It's easier that trying to remember all those hard names people call them."

"Alright, I will call them cow-lizards. So, we hid in the herd of cow-lizards," thought Teeg. "The toothies do not attack them when they are in a herd. That would be suicide! The only problem was those cow-lizards are not very smart, and for some reason they thought Dino was one of their babies. Maybe it was all the mud and leaves he was covered with."

"They are very protective of their young and they would not let Dino leave. We were trapped in the herd for days, until you found us." Teeg let out a big yawn. "I will let Dino finish the rest of the story. I am so tired. Those cow-lizard things snore so loud all night you cannot sleep!"

Teeg was exhausted from three days of no food and no sleep and was about to collapse.

"Thank you," thought Arbee. "You and Dino go get some sleep now, while the rest of us try to figure out how to get you back to your starship."

"Thank you," thought Teeg. He walked over, took another drink of water and then lay down on a nice soft pad next to Dino and Bootsey. It was not long before all three of them were in a deep sleep.

"All right everyone, we need to have an emergency meeting on the bridge, immediately," said Arbee in a serious voice.

Captain Cliven Greck stood at the entrance of his small, well-worn starship looking across the prehistoric landscape. His dark blue uniform ruffled quietly in the hot and dusty wind.

The Captain was a very large, muscular man who stood over six and a half feet tall. He had thick, dark hair and tan, leathery skin. There were faint scars on his face and arms from his long, hard career as a space explorer.

Space explorers, or 'spacers' as most people of this

time called them, had to be tough because space is an extremely dangerous environment – extreme hot, extreme cold, radiation, space pirates, hostile civilizations, ship breakdowns, exploding suns, meteors, asteroids and other floating space junk were just a few of the things that could wreck a ship and kill a 'spacer' in the blink of an eye.

"TEEG!" yelled Captain Greck, as he looked across the forest and fern-covered plains for his lost dog, the only other member of his crew. They had been attacked by a pack of diamond-back toothies, which is what Greck called the Allosaurs that roamed this uncivilized world.

Teeg had tricked the pack of meat-eating beasts into following him away from the ship.

The brave dog not only saved the ship, he had saved Greck as well.

Captain Greck had taken his rocket sled out many times in an attempt to find his friend without any luck.

Teeg had gone missing before, but he had always returned safely. Greck did not want to leave without him, but … he could not wait forever.

Back on the bridge of Arbee's starship, an important meeting with Zinzu and the Science Team was in progress.

"Science Team, we have a number of problems that we must solve before we can continue our research," said Arbee. "Problem number one is that we must get Teeg back to his ship without letting his owner, Captain Greck, know

we are here."

"How come?" asked Banjo. "Is Captain Greck dangerous?"

"Let me guess," said Lee. "If this guy sees us he will shoot us in the head, right?"

"Although Earth is an uncivilized planet during this time, there are a number of advanced human civilizations on other planets in this part of the galaxy," said Arbee. "As I have explained to you before, human beings are actually a very old body type and can be found throughout this part of the universe."

"The human empires in this area are extremely warlike and dangerous. That is one of the reasons time travelers are strictly forbidden to have any contact with them. Unfortunately, we found Captain Greck's lost dog by accident."

"Maybe we could take Teeg home with us," said Banjo. "I could probably talk my parents into letting me keep him. I'll tell them he is a stray or something."

"You can't take Teeg out of this time," said Lee. "Remember? He will disappear! Plus, he doesn't look like an Earth dog. You'd be busted in two seconds."

"Oh … yeah," sighed Banjo. "I thought maybe there was a way … never mind."

"I am sorry, Banjo," sighed Arbee. "I wish we could take Teeg back. It would make things easier. But we cannot."

"Arbee, I know you said that we can't mess up the

future by being back here in the past, but ... what about these space people or civilizations or whatever? Can they change our future because of their science?" asked Sam.

"We believe it is quite possible," explained Arbee. "We have never seen it happen, but people, unlike animals, might be able to change events so much that they overpower time and make the future turn out differently. That is why we cannot risk ANY kind of contact with Greck or any of his people."

"So if we run into this Greck guy," said Lee, "we could mess up the future so bad that we might not even be born?"

"As I said before, it is possible," Arbee replied. "If he decided to attack us, well, this is a research vessel, NOT a battleship. And if Captain Greck got hold of any of the information on this starship, with science that is millions of years ahead of his, there is no telling what would happen. It could be a disaster for the present and the future."

"Great! Just great!" grumbled Lee. "I don't know what's worse, getting eaten by an Allosaur or never being born. This is all Dino's fault, you dumb dog!"

"Shut up, Lee!" yelled Banjo. "Dino was DEFENDING us! He SAVED MY LIFE and probably yours, too!"

"CHILL OUT, YOU GUYS!" interrupted Sam. "Arguing is not going to help."

Zinzu floated over and spoke, "I just realized something important about all this!"

"And what is that?" asked Arbee.

"If Teeg had not found Dino and helped him by hiding out in the Stegosaurus herd, he most likely would have made it safely back to his ship," said Zinzu. "Dino was not supposed to be there, so by helping Teeg get back to his ship, where he is supposed to be ... we will not be disrupting the past. We will be repairing it!"

"Yes, Yes," said Arbee. "You are quite right, Zinzu."

"So, we have got to get Teeg back," added Sam, "without being detected and the future will come out okay. Does anyone have any ideas?"

"Well ... why don't we turn on the shuttle's camouflage, fly out, land it behind this Greck guy's ship, drop Teeg off, and then fly out of there ... WHOOSH," said Lee.

"Great idea," said Arbee. "Except that Greck's starship has sensors that can see right through the shuttle's camouflage. We would be ..."

"Sitting ducks," interrupted Lee. "Then we'd be dead ducks!"

"Could we jam his ship's sensors?" asked Sam. "Or shut them down for a while. I mean just long enough to get Teeg back?"

"We could jam his sensors," said Zinzu, "but Greck would see that they were being jammed and think he was under attack. He would come looking for us with his blast cannons blazing. I believe it would be too risky."

"Agreed," said Arbee.

"Just how advanced is this guy's science and

equipment?" asked Lee.

"It is as advanced as some space civilizations are now," said Arbee, "and very dangerous."

Just then, Dino came out of the kitchen and walked slowly over to Arbee with his ears back and his tail between his legs.

He sat down on the floor in front of Arbee and looked up at him with his big, brown Chow-Chow eyes. He was obviously very sad. He had heard everything that was said during the meeting.

"I am sorry," thought Dino. "I didn't mean to cause so much trouble. I feel so bad, but it's my job to protect Banjo from enemies."

Arbee gently patted Dino. "Do not feel bad," he thought. "You did your job and helped save us from the bird dinosaurs. I do not want you to blame yourself." Arbee told the others what Dino was thinking.

Banjo went over to Dino and hugged him. "It's okay, buddy," he whispered. "You are the best. Besides, how were you supposed to know that some alien spaceman had landed his ship nearby?"

Dino wagged his tail and licked Banjo's freckled face. It made Banjo laugh.

Sam elbowed Lee. "Apologize to Dino," she said in an angry whisper. "Now!"

Lee sighed, "I am sorry, Dino, for calling you dumb."

"You all forget something else," added Sam. "If Dino

had not run into Teeg, we would not have known about Cliven Greck. Then WE would have run into him and — ZAP — that would be the end of us and maybe the future. My mom says that things happen for a reason."

"Samantha is quite right," added Zinzu.

"Well, Dino, it looks like this is the second time you have saved us on this trip," said Arbee, "without us even knowing it! However, we still need a solution to our problem and we must find it fast, before Greck takes off and leaves poor Teeg behind."

Dino was feeling much better now. He jumped up and whapped Arbee with his big paw. "I have got an idea!" he thought. "I know a place where we can land the shuttle, drop Teeg off and if you do it right ... Captain Greck will never know we were ever there!"

Chapter Eight
OPERATION ... SNEAKY STEGOSAURS

It was now late afternoon out on the dusty red plain, bordered by a thick fern and redwood tree forest. The sea of bright green ferns and other bushes which covered the ground were swaying back and forth in the soft warm breeze.

Nearby, a herd of Stegosaurs of all sizes was grazing on the tender plants, nipping them off with their beak-like mouths.

The different shades of green that covered the Stegosaurs' bodies made them look like large, slow-moving camouflaged tanks. Some of them were fifteen feet high and over twenty feet long.

The herd had been moving in an easterly direction for most of the day, being led by a new addition to the group ... a large, old male Stegosaurus.

He seemed to know where he was going, and for some

reason, the other Stegosaurs felt that they had to follow him. They did not really care where they were going as long as there was plenty of food.

The herd had been moving along without any problem, until they passed near a very thick part of the forest.

Without warning, two young Allosaurs charged from the forest's edge and tried to grab a young female Stegosaur who had wandered a little too far from the protection of the herd.

The response from the adult Stegosaurs was quick. A group of them charged the Allosaurs with their deadly spiked tails raised high in the air, like giant prehistoric scorpions.

They then did something that was rare in the world of dinosaurs, something that modern day paleontologists could not have discovered from fossil bones.

The tall plates that went down the middle of the backs of the angry Stegosaurs suddenly turned a bright red.

They were like oversized prehistoric chameleons, able to change colors when they were threatened.

As the Stegosaurs moved closer toward the meat-eaters, they vibrated their colorful plates much like a bird ruffles its feathers and that made a loud rattling sound.

At the same time they started hissing so loudly it sounded like the noise made by a jet airplane.

The young Allosaurs were so confused and frightened by all the noise and the bright red color on the Stegosaurs that they stopped their attack.

One of the large male Stegosaurs charged in closer to the Allosaurs. He rose up on his powerful hind legs and, as he came back down on all fours, he swung his deadly spiked tail around and – WHOOSH – just barely missed one of the Allosaurs, nearly knocking it over.

The Allosaurs, realizing that this was no place to get a meal, turned tail and retreated back to the safety of the thick forest. They had learned a valuable lesson … NEVER attack Stegosaurs when they are in a herd … EVER!

The adult Stegosaurs remained on guard with their spiked tails ready to fight until they were sure the danger had passed. Then their color returned to normal and one by one they returned to the herd, making sure that the wandering young female was pushed back in with them.

The herd continued on their way, following the old Stegosaurus toward a strange dark object up ahead.

"Awesome!" whispered Banjo. "Arbee, did you see what those Stegosaurs did?"

"Yes, it was amazing," replied Arbee, "They are interesting creatures, these Stegosaurs. Quite different from other dinosaurs we have studied."

"Paleontologists never dreamed these dinosaurs could change colors and rattle their plates," said Banjo. "I mean, they have got a brain the size of a walnut. They are supposed to be one of the dumbest dinosaurs ever."

"Yes, but you forget," said Arbee, "according to your computer dinosaur book, Stegosaurs were very successful. There were a number of different types that lived all around this planet. Once we get Teeg back to his ship we must find out why."

Arbee and Banjo, along with Sam, Bootsey, Dino and Lee, had been watching the Stegosaurs and Allosaurs battle from the safety of Arbee's shuttle craft.

Arbee had taken Dino's suggestion for the perfect place to hide so they could get close to Cliven Greck's starship without being spotted.

That place was right in the middle of the Stegosaur herd.

Banjo had suggested to Arbee that he should make the shuttle look like a big Stegosaurus, so Arbee did just that. By using electronic screens he made the ship look like a big male Stegosaurus.

It took some time for them to figure out how to do it but the disguise worked perfectly.

A few of the big males tried to stop the fake Stegosaurus shuttle when it entered the herd but Arbee convinced them to let him in with a few harmless zaps from one of the shuttle's weapons.

Then, by using push and pull energy beams, Arbee was able to direct the herd toward Greck's starship, which was now less than five hundred feet away.

"We will move just a little closer," said Arbee. "Then we will let you out, Teeg, and you will have to make a run for to your ship."

"I am ready anytime," thought Teeg to Arbee. "I can make it."

"Let's hope the new screen that Zinzu invented will block Greck's sensors," said Sam.

"Too bad we didn't have time to test it," added Banjo.

"Yeah, well ... keep your fingers crossed," sighed Sam."It worked back at the ship."

"If that Greck guy starts shooting at us, I am out of here," mumbled Lee. "I'll take my chances with the Stegosaurus herd."

The disguised shuttle moved with the herd, closer and closer toward the black starship.

Captain Greck had been working on his ship all day, testing plant, soil and mineral samples in the ship's laboratory.

He had been keeping a close eye on the herd of 'spiky tails' that had been moving toward his ship all afternoon, but now the stomping, rattling and mooing sounds of the herd were louder than ever.

He stopped what he was doing, walked over to the ship's weapons cabinet, unlocked it and took out a large Model Thirty-two Blast Rifle. He put in a power cartridge and walked out the hatch of his ship, where he could see the dinosaurs which were now only three hundred feet away.

"Those air-for-brains 'spiky tails'!" he thought to himself. "They are getting too close. I'll have to fire a few warning shots into the ground in front of them to drive them off. I sure wish Teeg was here. He would take care of those pests."

Greck did not want to kill any of the animals, not because he cared for them, but because he knew that if he blasted any of them that their dead bodies would attract every meat-eater for miles around, like the diamond-back toothies, horn-nosed toothies and at least a dozen others that he did not have names for.

And that was the last thing he needed right now.

Greck raised the heavy blast rifle and took careful aim at the ground, hoping his shots would cause the dinosaur herd to stampede in the other direction and away from his ship.

He clicked a switch on the side of the weapon from "OFF" to "FIRE", placed his finger on the trigger, and was about to shoot when he heard something ... a familiar sound.

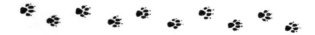

Teeg was up on his hind legs looking through the shuttle's glass top as it moved closer to his home, the starship.

He saw his owner, Captain Cliven Greck, step out of the ship holding a large blast rifle. "Oh, no!" he thought to Arbee. "Arbee, stop the herd! Stop them now or we are all dead!"

Arbee, who had also seen Greck holding a weapon, immediately stopped the ship. "Samantha, turn off all the push-pull beams, quickly!"

"Okay," she replied, – CLICK, CLICK, CLICK – Sam pushed the buttons on her control board, turning off all the beams. "Done," she said.

The shuttle and the herd stopped moving forward.

"Holy cows, the spaceman guy has got some kind of a gun and he is pointing it right at us! I think he is going to shoot at the Stegosaurs!" warned Lee.

"Arbee you must let me out now!" thought Teeg. "I can save you, but I must go now!"

"All right," thought Arbee to Teeg. Arbee turned to Banjo and said, "Banjo, we need to let Teeg out. On my signal open the hatch!"

"Got it," replied Banjo, who put his hand on the 'Open Hatch' button at the rear of the shuttle.

Arbee lowered the shuttle to the ground. "Ready ... now Banjo!" he said.

WHAP – Banjo hit the button and – SWOOSH – the door opened.

"Bye, Teeg!" thought Dino. "Thanks for helping me."

"Good luck," thought Bootsey. "Say hello to the cats on your planet or whatever you call them."

"Thank you and a safe journey to you all," thought Teeg. He barked a farewell to the others and was out the door in a flash.

"Bye, Teeg," whispered Banjo. "Thanks for saving Dino." – WHAP – Banjo closed the shuttle's hatch.

Everyone ran to the front of the shuttle hoping Teeg would stop Cliven Greck from firing his blast rifle at the herd of Stegosaurs.

"Look at how fast he is running," said Banjo.

"He is the fastest dog I have ever seen," thought Dino. "See, he even got past that cow-lizard."

"Hurry up Teeg," said Lee. "I don't want to get shot."

Teeg made it out of the herd and started barking as loud as he could, "ARF, ARF, ARF!"

But, Greck was still pointing his weapon at the Stegosaurs and the shuttle.

"He is not lowering his gun yet," said Sam.

"I wonder if he knows we are here," said Lee.

Chapter Nine
RUN, TEEG, RUN!

Captain Greck was about to open fire at the herd of Stegosaurs when he heard a faint and familiar sound. He took his finger off the trigger but did not lower his blast rifle.

He noticed something running out of the herd at an amazing speed. It was brown and black and "Is it barking?" he thought.

Greck looked through the target sight of his rifle and pushed the 'magnify' button to get a better look. He could not believe what he saw.

"TEEG, HERE TEEG … COME ON BOY!" he yelled. Cliven Greck was not a man who smiled much, but now he was grinning like a kid with a candy bar.

His dog Teeg was alive and coming home.

"Samantha, turn on the push-pull beams again," said

Arbee, "but this time put them in reverse. Teeg is almost back to his ship and it is time we retreated, before we are found out."

CLICK, CLICK, CLICK – Sam turned on the beams and – CLICK – put them in reverse. "Beams are on and in reverse," she said.

"Good," replied Arbee. "Here we go." Slowly, he turned around and flew the shuttle craft backward away from Greck's starship.

The Stegosaur herd turned at the same time and followed the shuttle, which was still disguised as the old Stegosaurus.

The herd continued eating plants and went on as if nothing had happened.

Lee, who was still watching Teeg run toward his ship, suddenly gasped, "Arbee, an Allosaur is after Teeg. He is trying to eat him!"

Arbee looked up from his controls. "Yes, I see it," he said. "This is a bad time for an Allosaur attack, a bad time indeed."

"Run, Teeg!" whispered Sam. "You've got to hurry!"

"Arbee, can you shoot it," asked Banjo, "without that Greck guy seeing you?"

"I am working on it," said Arbee. He quickly turned on the shuttle's weapons system and targeted the Allosaur.

He was trying to figure out how to shoot the dinosaur without being spotted.

Dino was thinking of whapping the 'Open' button on the shuttle's hatch with his paw and running out to help Teeg.

"Do not even think about it!" thought Arbee to Dino. "You let me handle this."

Dino just snorted and went over to the other side of the shuttle to look out through the glass. He felt angry.

A Chow Chow dog always goes to the defense of his friends, but now all he could do was watch poor Teeg fight for his life.

Dino's only hope was that Teeg remembered what he had taught him about fighting those big bird-lizards.

Cliven Greck's smile vanished when he saw a diamond-back toothy attack Teeg from behind a nearby hill of bushes and boulders.

The attack happened so fast that he had not been able to react quickly enough.

Teeg was smarter and faster than the Allosaur. Instantly he dove behind a large rock – SNAP – Teeg was nearly crushed by the Allosaur's snapping jaws and dagger-like teeth.

The quick thinking dog danced around the protective boulder staying one step ahead of the hungry dinosaur, but he could not keep doing this forever.

Cliven Greck went into an angry rage and ran as fast

as his powerful legs would make him go, directly toward his dog's attacker, yelling at the top of his lungs, "HEY, HEY, TOOTHY, OVER HERE! LOOK OVER HERE!"

Greck's loud, booming voice got the Allosaur's attention. It stopped going after Teeg and looked over at him, which is exactly what the Captain had hoped would happen.

In less than one second, Greck dropped down to the ground on one knee, aimed his blast rifle and fired a carefully aimed shot – BOOM – at the Allosaur's massive head.

WHAP – the Allosaur did not even get a chance to react before he was hit with a powerful blast of white light.

It burned a perfect two-inch hole all the way through its thick skull.

The stunned dinosaur paused for a few seconds, then, its lifeless body flopped to the ground – THUD – in a cloud of red dust and fern leaves.

Teeg, seeing that the dinosaur was dead, wasted no time running as fast as he could straight to Cliven Greck.

"Good boy, Teeg," yelled Greck. "Come on, boy!"

But instead of leaping into Greck's arms, Teeg ran right past his confused owner barking like a crazy dog. Greck turned around and saw what Teeg was going after.

Another Allosaur was attacking him from behind! Before the startled Captain could raise his blast rifle to fire a shot at the charging animal, Teeg ran up to it, leaped high into the air and grabbed the surprised Allosaur by the skin on its stomach.

It roared loudly as the angry dog shook as hard as he could, sinking his wolf-like teeth deeper and deeper into the Allosaur's flesh.

Then something totally unexpected happened. Greck thought he heard a low – THUMP – sound and the Allosaur, who had been jumping around trying to shake Teeg loose, stopped moving and immediately dropped to the ground – THUD.

Teeg let go of the dinosaur and backed away. He barked at it, "GARF, ARF, GARF, GARF," waiting for it to attack again but it just lay there.

Greck ran up and poked it with the end of his blast rifle. The Allosaur was not dead, but it was totally knocked out!

"Hah!" thought Teeg. "Dino was right! Biting toothies on the stomach really works."

"What … Teeg?" said Cliven Greck, amazed, "How did you do that? You knocked out a toothy. You must have hit some kind of nerve or something. Good boy!"

"GARF, ARF!" barked Teeg. "It's a little trick I learned from a friend," he thought.

But Greck, like most humans, was not very good at reading thoughts, so Teeg ran up and licked him on the face. Greck laughed as he hugged his dog. "It's good to see you too, you old space bum. Now let's have a look at you. Where in the blazing suns have you been? Your coat is clean and shiny. You look more like you've been on vacation instead of running around the woods for three days." Then Greck looked Teeg in the eyes. "You've been up to something haven't you, you old mutt."

"Grrr, arf!" replied Teeg. "Sorry, cannot tell you, Captain," he thought. "It is top secret."

"Hmmm, wish I could understand dog talk," said Greck. "No matter, it's time we get off this miserable monster-infested planet before that toothy wakes up and realizes I blasted its friend into the next life!"

"This is no place for humans or dogs anyway, not unless the Department of New Colonies can figure out how to wipe out all of these toothies, long-necks and spiky- tails," said Greck, "and besides, we are overdue at base camp for more food and supplies. We have only enough food for two more days, after that we will have to eat roast toothy for dinner."

"Garf!" barked Teeg. "Yuck, trust me," he thought, "toothies taste bad. I am ready to leave when you are!"

Cliven Greck and his dog Teeg climbed aboard their battered starship. Greck closed and locked the outer hatch. After he and Teeg ate a quick meal, Greck made preparations for take off.

The starship's take off rockets fired, sending a loud thundering noise across the plains and raising a huge cloud of dirt, dust and smoke into the late afternoon sky.

As the ship rose into the air, Greck set a course for the fourth planet in the same solar system. They were going to a planet which had life on it, but was much safer than Earth.

The planet's name on the star charts was simply 'P4/SZ08301'. One hundred and forty million years in the future the planet would be given a different name. It would be called – Mars. It was named after the ancient Roman god of war because of its fiery red color.

"Nice shot, Arbee!" said Banjo as he and the others watched the second Allosaur fall to the ground.

"That was awesome. Did you kill it?" asked Lee.

"No, no," replied Arbee. "I just knocked it out. It will sleep for hours. That should be plenty of time for Captain Greck and Teeg to get their ship ready for blast off."

"Arf!" barked Dino. "I could have stopped that bird-lizard," he thought.

"Dino, I do not doubt that. But you have chased enough dinosaurs on this trip," thought Arbee.

Dino just sighed and lay down next to Bootsey. "People don't understand Chow Chow dogs," he thought to Bootsey.

"Well, what did you expect?" thought Bootsey. "You take off for three days and everyone has to stop everything they are doing and run all over the place looking for YOU. I had to skip at least FIVE naps helping them find you. You are lucky a CAT was here to save you."

Dino just sighed again and scratched his ear.

"But don't feel so bad," thought Bootsey. "You dogs never think about what you are doing, you just go, go, go and you end up in trouble. We cats plan out everything we do. You could learn a thing or two about life from a cat."

Dino sighed once again, "Humph, now I am being yelled at by a cat," he thought. "What is this world coming to?"

"Well, this has been an interesting day," said Sam. "Now, let's hope this guy takes off and leaves without figuring out that it was Arbee and not Teeg who knocked out that Allosaur."

"Speaking of which," said Arbee, "Looks like the starship's rockets are firing. If all goes as planned, this should all be over soon."

They all watched as the starship's blast off rockets fired.

"Those rockets sure are loud," shouted Lee, who was covering his ears with his hands. "Look at all the dust and stuff. Should we be this close? I don't think we should be this close."

"Hey, Arbee, I think Lee maybe right," said Banjo. "Are you sure we are far enough away?"

But before Arbee could answer, flying rock and plants from the rocket's blast engines were hitting the glass of the shuttle craft and the herd of Stegosaurs.

The shower of rocks along with the ear-splitting noise and shaking ground, made the Stegosaurs move away faster and faster. The adults let out loud honking calls, which was a Stegosaur signal to ... STAMPEDE!

Chapter Ten
THE NEW WEAPON

"Samantha, turn off the push-pull beams immediately," yelled Arbee, "or we will be dragged with the herd and they will wreck the shuttle!"

Sam's fingers moved quickly across the computer control board, shutting off the beams just in time — CLICK, CLICK – "Done!" she yelled over the loud noise of the stampeding Stegosaurs.

"Hang on to something, everyone!" yelled Arbee as he carefully piloted the shuttle craft to keep up with the herd. "This is going to be a rough ride!" he yelled. "But we have no choice! We must stay hidden until I am sure we have not been detected by Captain Greck's starship."

And it was a rough ride. They were bumped and bounced, back and forth, by the panicky Stegosaurs.

Banjo held onto Dino so that the dog would not be thrown against the side of the shuttle craft. "This is the worst car ride ever," thought Dino.

"I think I am going to be sick," groaned Lee, who was holding onto his stomach with one hand while holding onto the side of the shuttle with the other. He was getting a bad case of motion sickness.

"Don't barf on me," scolded Banjo. "Don't BARF at all because you will stink up the whole place and then you will make everyone else barf!"

"Hold on, Lee. It should not be too much longer," assured Arbee. "Look straight ahead out the front of the ship. That should help to calm your stomach."

Arbee tried to work the shuttle's controls to make the ride smoother, which helped.

Banjo was watching the Stegosaurs running and noticed that they did not gallop like horses, they ran like elephants and their tails did not drag on the ground like some of the old dinosaur books showed. They held them up in the air. Then he noticed something else...

"Hey, check it out!" yelled Banjo. "The Stegos are changing color ... even the babies!"

Everywhere they looked the Science Team could see hundreds of bright red, red orange fins on the Stegosaurs' backs as they moved through thick clouds of reddish brown dust.

Far in front of the panicky herd Banjo could see dinosaurs of all kinds running. They were trying to keep from being trampled to death and get out of the way of the wall of charging Stegosaurs.

Finally, after what seemed like forever, the Stegosaur

herd began to slow down.

Their brightly colored backs and fins began to fade back to their normal blotchy green color. Then they stopped and rested for a while.

One by one the Stegosaurs went back to the endless job of eating lots of tender green ferns, as if nothing had happened.

"Man, it's about time. This is why I do not ride roller coasters," said Lee as he lay on the shuttle's floor trying to get his head to stop spinning and his upset stomach to calm down.

Dino walked over to Lee. "Here, this should help," he thought, and started to lick Lee's face.

"HEY, quit that, Dino," Lee complained. "That is totally GROSS! You clean yourself with that tongue. You are going to make me throw up for sure!"

"Don't be such a wimp," thought Dino. "It's only dog spit and it's good for you because it makes you feel better."

Banjo and Sam laughed while Bootsey just cleaned himself. "Silly dog," thought Bootsey. "That's what you get for trying to help people."

Arbee flew over to Lee. "How are you feeling, Lee?" he asked.

"Better," Lee grunted, "now that Dino quit slobbering on me."

"Well thank you for not throwing up in the shuttle craft," said Arbee. "It would have been quite messy. Zinzu would not be happy. Sometimes I forget that your bodies are full of all sorts of liquids and things."

"No problem," moaned Lee. "Can we go back to the ship now? I am starving."

"Starving? A few minutes ago you were about to throw up all over the place!" exclaimed Banjo.

"That was THEN, and this is NOW!" explained Lee. "Almost getting shot by aliens and smashed to bits by stampeding Stegosaurs has made me hungry."

"Unbelievable!" mumbled Banjo, shaking his head.

"Let me see if it is safe to return to the starship," said Arbee. He pushed the radio button on the shuttle's control board. "Arbee to Zinzu, come in please."

"Zinzu here, how goes Operation Teeg?"

"Mission accomplished," answered Arbee. "Zinzu, I need you to check the deep space sensors. I need to know where Cliven Greck's vessel is located at this moment."

"Understood, I am searching now. Please stand by," said Zinzu. After a short time he came back, "Deep space search is complete. It shows that there are no other ships anywhere near Earth and Greck's ship has just entered into orbit around the planet Mars."

"Excellent. We are returning to the starship, Arbee out."

"I will make preparations, Zinzu out,"

"It is time we left our Stegosaur friends," said Arbee. "When we get back to the ship you can get cleaned up, eat and rest."

"This has been the craziest three days of my life," said Banjo who looked very tired.

"Same with me," thought Dino. "At least you didn't have to spend three days with those cow-lizards."

"Now that the Teeg problem is solved," continued Arbee, "we will need to continue our meeting and solve some other important problems. We are not done with this yet."

Arbee floated, with his arms folded, in front of a well fed and rested Science Team. Zinzu floated near Arbee.

Sitting on the floor of the ship's bridge, between Arbee and the Science Team, was a strange green box.

Arbee spoke, "Now that Teeg is back where he belongs and the time line has been corrected, we must resolve the next problem."

"What's that?" asked Banjo. "You're not kicking us out are you?"

"No, not at all," said Arbee. "However, we must solve the problem of SELF DEFENSE."

"Self defense?" asked Banjo, "but we have our sling shots with the flash marbles ..."

"They are practically useless," interrupted Arbee. "You see, this whole mess started when we were attacked by all of those feathered dinosaurs at once."

"We did fight them off," said Banjo, "well ... sort of."

"Yeah, but we almost didn't," said Lee. "I could not load my sling shot fast enough. I had to kick a couple of them in the head! We almost got eaten. Anyway, Arbee is right. These sling shots are useless when there is a bunch of dinosaurs attacking us."

"Lee is right," said Sam. We are lucky to be alive."

"Yeah," Banjo sighed, "I see what you are saying. If I had not had my backpack on I would have been shredded by that crazy Birdosaur."

"Exactly," said Arbee. "And so, after some research, Zinzu and I have arrived at a solution. We discovered that people on your planet play a popular sport called 'Paintball'."

"Yeah, so, oh, wait ... you made us paintball guns?" asked Banjo.

Arbee lifted the lid off the green box. Everyone gathered around. "Have a look," he said, "brand new Paintball guns. These Paintball guns are much better than anything you can get on Earth."

"Ummm ... okay," said Lee, "exactly how are we going to stop DINOSAURS with PAINT?"

"Not PAINT, silly!" explained Arbee. "These Paintball guns shoot the flash marbles I designed for your sling shots."

"Ohhhh, now I get it," said Lee. "What a GREAT IDEA!"

"These are cool, Arbee," whispered Sam. "This will work so much better."

"Awesome!" said Banjo. "I would like to see those Birdosaurs charge us now."

"Trouble," thought Bootsey. "Children with weapons ... this cannot be good."

"Any of you people shoot me with those guns and I will personally POOP in your SHOES," thought Dino.

"Go ahead, each of you take one," said Arbee.

Banjo, Lee and Sam each took one of the green guns out of the box. Zinzu floated over and took the box away.

"They are nice and light," said Lee, lifting the Paintball gun up and down.

"The weapons were made to be light and compact. They have a strap so that they can be easily carried over your shoulder and they have two hand grips ... one in the front and one in the back where the trigger is," explained Arbee.

"How do you load it?" asked Banjo, looking it over.

Arbee took the weapon from Banjo and pushed a button on the front of the gun below the barrel. A small hatch popped open. "Just put the flash marbles in here. It holds over a hundred flash marbles. Then close it. You see? Simple," he said. "You just aim and shoot."

"Oh yeah, I see," said Banjo. "This is great. How far does it shoot?"

"It has an effective distance of three hundred feet," added Arbee. "It is powered by a battery pack, not air like the Paintball guns from Earth. The battery pack will last for six years. But there is one important thing you must remember. Repeat after me – 'THIS IS NOT A TOY'!"

Sam, Lee and Banjo repeated, "THIS IS NOT A TOY."

"Good," replied Arbee. "ANYONE violating this rule will be removed from the Science Team forever and there are NO exceptions. Do I make myself clear?"

"Yes!" they replied, nodding their heads. They had never seen Arbee so serious before. They definitely got the message – DO NOT play around with these guns or you will be OUT!

"All right," said Arbee, "before we go out to study the Stegosaurs again, Banjo, you and Lee go with Zinzu. He will teach you how to use these new weapons correctly and safely."

"Come along," said Zinzu. The boys followed Zinzu to another deck of the ship with their new Paintball guns.

"Samantha, I need your assistance." said Arbee. "We are going to solve the last problem and that is our friend Dino."

"Okay," said Sam, "but I am not sure what I can do to help."

"Oh great. What did I do now?" thought Dino. "I am in big trouble."

"Dino, you and I need to talk," said Arbee. "First, I want to know what happened while you stayed with the herd of Stegosaurs. It is valuable research. And second, we need to review your fighting methods. You left Banjo unprotected when you ran into the woods after the Birdosaurs and got yourself lost and almost killed."

"Okay," thought Dino. "Are you going to yell at me or hit me with a rolled-up newspaper?"

"Yelling … Hitting?" asked Arbee. "What nonsense! Is that how dogs are treated on your planet?"

"Yeah, a lot of dogs, well … most of them are," thought Dino. "Some dogs are treated better than others. But Banjo and his family treat me well, except the little sister, Cassie."

"Well, there will be no hitting or yelling on this ship," thought Arbee. He turned to Sam. "Samantha, please go to the computer and look up as much information as you can about Chow Chow dogs? I want to know about their history such as where they came from, what they were used for and anything else you can find.

"Okay. Chow Chow dog history," replied Sam. "I can do that." She walked over to a computer on the side of the bridge and went to work. "I'll let you know what I find, Arbee."

"Thank you," said Arbee, "and while you do that I will find out what happened to our friend here."

Arbee turned to Dino. "All right, Dino, what happened when you chased those bird dinosaurs into the woods?" Arbee thought, "And how did you end up with the Stegosaurs?"

Dino sat down and sighed. "Well, Teeg told you some of what happened but he left out a lot. So here is the rest of the story."

Chapter Eleven
WHAT HAPPENED TO DINO?

Dino began to tell Arbee the story of his adventure with the Stegosaurs by sending Arbee his thoughts. "Well, after I knocked down those two bird-lizard things ..."

"Birdosaurs," thought Arbee. "We do not know what they are, so we are calling them Birdosaurs for now."

"Okay," thought Dino. "So I knocked down those Birdosaurs to keep them from eating Banjo, but they got up and ran toward the forest. I wanted to make sure they were not going to attack us again, so I went after them. Just like I thought, one of the Birdosaurs turned and tried to ATTACK me!"

"They are very dangerous creatures," thought Arbee.

"You mean they are CRAZY. Even worse than CATS!" thought Dino. "But I bit it in the throat and, well, I guess you found its body in the forest."

"Yes, we did," thought Arbee. "For a moment, we thought that it might have been you."

"No way, they might be mean, but they are not as tough as me," thought Dino. "So I chased after the second Birdosaur all the way to the edge of that big swamp. All of a sudden it turned and tried to JUMP on my head and BITE my face, so I flipped it to the ground and killed it. I do not like those things! They make me mad."

"Is that the Birdosaur that you ate?" thought Arbee.

"Huh?" thought Dino. "You think I ate it?"

"Yes," thought Arbee. "We found the creature's body next to the swamp, partially eaten."

"No," thought Dino. "I didn't eat it. Besides, those dinosaurs may look like birds but they sure don't taste like them. They smell like dirty socks and taste like an old shoe that's been left in a closet for too long. Know what I mean?"

"I have never eaten a dirty sock or an old shoe from a closet," thought Arbee, "but I will take your word for it. Please continue."

"Okay, after that I tried to get back to Banjo and the rest of the Science Team," continued Dino, "and guess what I ran into?"

"What?" asked Arbee.

"One of those big meat-eater bird-lizards with the fin or horn on its nose," Dino replied.

"You mean a Ceratosaur?" thought Arbee.

"Yeah, that's what Banjo called it. I call them bird-lizards," thought Dino. "We ran into them a few trips ago. What a pain in the tail those things are. So I turned and started running along the edge of the big swamp to escape it when all of a sudden one of those ... Allo ... Alla ..."

"Do you mean an Allosaur?" thought Arbee.

"I think so," thought Dino. "Is it the bird-lizard that has colors like a big reddish-orange rattlesnake?

"That is the one," thought Arbee.

"Well, this Allosaur bird-lizard LEAPT right in front of me and tried to BITE me but I was too fast for him," thought Dino. "So I dove into some thick bushes in the forest to escape."

Luckily, the Allosaur bird-lizard saw the Ceratosaur bird-lizard and started chasing after it," he thought. "That gave me enough time to run through the forest and circle back to the swamp."

"I ran through the water to hide my tracks and scent from the bird-lizard. That is an old dog trick." Dino thought. "People say they invented it, but they learned it from dogs."

"Hmmm, I was told that cats invented that trick," thought Arbee.

"CATS, hah ... no way!" thought Dino. "Cats are liars. I am telling you dogs invented it. Anyway, so I ran through the swamp," he continued, "as fast as I could to put some distance between me and those bird-lizards. Then I turned into the forest to get back to where you guys were. But instead of turning into the forest, I went PLOP!"

"PLOP?" asked Arbee.

"Yes, PLOP," replied Dino. "I fell right into this big

pit full of sticky, smelly swamp mud and big leaves and I got completely covered with all kinds of jungle garbage. I looked like a walking bush."

"We missed that when we were tracking you. It sounds messy," thought Arbee.

"Yes it was," thought Dino, "and what was worse is that it took me forever to climb out of the slimy pit because the sides were so slippery."

Finally, I got out and kept running along the swamp for a while then I turned into the forest again because I am still trying to get back to you guys. So, I was going through the woods and guess what I ran into then?" asked Dino.

"What?" asked Arbee.

"Allosaur bird-lizards," thought Dino. "Not one but FIVE!"

"Oh, that is not good," thought Arbee.

"No it was not good," thought Dino. "So, I ran back to the swamp AGAIN, with all those hungry bird-lizards chasing me."

"Ah ha," thought Arbee, "those were the meat-eater tracks I saw near your footprints."

"Yes and you probably thought I was dead, didn't you?" thought Dino.

"Let us just say that you had us worried," thought Arbee.

"Well, I was not dead. I ran like crazy," thought Dino,

"which was not easy with all that mud and junk all over me."

"It must have been very difficult," thought Arbee.

"You bet it was difficult," he thought, "but don't forget ... I also had FIVE bird-lizards right on my tail."

"Unbelievable!" thought Arbee.

"You think THAT was unbelievable," thought Dino, "while I ran along I looked ahead of me and guess what I saw this time?"

"You saw another Allosaur," thought Arbee, "or a Ceratosaur?"

"No," replied Dino. "Right there, standing by the swamp was another DOG!"

"Oh, that must be when you found Teeg, correct?" thought Arbee.

"Yes, it was Teeg," thought Dino, "and he told me to follow him. So, I either follow this strange dog or I get chewed to pieces by five bird-lizards. I trust dogs a lot more than those bird-lizards, so, I went with Teeg."

"Excellent choice, I think," thought Arbee. "What happened next?"

"Teeg and me make a quick turn away from the swamp and into the forest," thought Dino. "Teeg led me through all these rocks and bushes. They were so confusing nothing could ever catch us."

"Teeg was a genius at escaping," Dino thought. "We got away from the bird-lizards and Teeg said to keep following him. He had a good hiding place where no 'toothy' could catch us. 'Toothy' is what Teeg called bird-lizards."

"Yes, I remember," thought Arbee. "It describes them quite well."

"So then me and Teeg ran through the forest until we got to the end of it. Then we ran out to the big valley and Teeg ran straight for the cow-lizards. You know the ones with the long horns on their tails."

"Stegosaurs," thought Arbee. "We just call them Stegos. It is easier."

"Yes, those things," thought Dino, "So, I say to Teeg …'Teeg, are you nuts? Those things will kill us the same as the bird-lizards. But Teeg says 'just trust me, we'll be safe with those things'. Well, it's a good thing I followed Teeg because just then those bird-lizards came out of the woods and started chasing us … AGAIN!"

"They do not give up easily," thought Arbee.

"They are PESTS," thought Dino. "Okay, so, we ran like crazy to the cow-lizard herd and Teeg was right because the cow-lizards did not attack us. They went straight for the bird-lizards with their spiky tails swinging and their back plates rattling, making all kinds of noises."

"Those bird-lizards turned tail and took off. They did not want ANYTHING to do with the angry cow-lizards and their spiky tails," thought Dino.

"I can see why. It is quite a sight to see the Stegosaurs fight," thought Arbee, "most frightening. What did you do after that?"

"We ran to the middle of the herd where the babies were," thought Dino, "because that was the safest part."

"Why do you think the Stegosaurs let you come into the herd?" asked Arbee.

"Teeg thought it was because of all the mud and big leaves all over me. It made me look like a baby cow-lizard."

Arbee laughed, "You mentioned that before."

"Yeah, it was funny, until me and Teeg found out those cow-lizards do not let their babies out of their sight," thought Dino. "That is why we couldn't escape. Even Teeg couldn't get out and that dog is even faster than me, or maybe he just stayed to help me … I am not sure."

"Anyway, the cow-lizards may seem stupid on their own, but when they are in a herd they have figured out a way to work together to make themselves smarter. They have a secret," thought Dino.

"A secret?" thought Arbee. He became very interested in this part of Dino's story. He knew that even though Stegosaurs were not very smart, they were still very successful and that living in herds was part of their success. But it was not the only reason.

"Tell me Dino, what do you think the Stegosaurs' secret is?' Arbee asked Dino.

"Sounds," thought Dino.

"Sounds?" asked Arbee. "But I did not hear them make that many sounds, just the usual grunts, moos and snorts."

"Sounds only DOGS can hear," said Dino. "High

sounds and low sounds. They use them to talk to each other and work together like … like …"

"Like whales," thought Arbee, "or a herd of elephants. They use sounds no one can hear, to talk to each other."

"Well, I have never seen whales or elephants, but I do not think that those cow-lizards are as smart as elephants or whales," thought Dino. But they are like a bunch of … not so smart animals working together to be … a bigger, smarter animal. Get it?"

"Yes, I do get it. That is how they survive," thought Arbee. "Very clever and YOU discovered it. Without your excellent dog ears I may never have figured this out."

"No problem," thought Dino. "Chows can do science, sometimes. Anyway, it's a good thing you rescued me and Teeg when you did because there was nothing to eat around there except plants – YUCK – and worst of all, those cow-lizards SNORE even worse than Banjo's grandpa after he eats a big dinner."

"It sounds horrible," thought Arbee, who was not sure what Dino meant.

"It was horrible," thought Dino. "We would have either starved to death or gone crazy from no sleep."

"Excuse me, Arbee," said Sam, who had just walked over.

"Yes, Samantha," said Arbee.

"Here is the 'History of Chow Chow Dogs' you asked for," she said, handing Arbee what looked like a small plastic disk. "Can I go practice shooting these new Paintball guns now with Lee and Banjo? I need to learn how to use them," she added, as she carefully picked up her weapon and looked it over.

"Oh, yes," replied Arbee. "Good idea. And thank you for the research."

"No problem," said Sam.

"When you are all finished with practice," said Arbee, "have everyone meet me back here on the bridge, all right?"

"Okay, I'll tell them," said Sam as she ran to the ship's elevator to join Lee, Banjo and Zinzu down on deck three.

Arbee took the disk Sam had given him and inserted it into a slot on his chest. "Now I shall see the history of Chow Chow dogs," he said "Interesting, very interesting."

"What does it say?" thought Dino. "Is it bad?"

Chapter Twelve
A PROMISE IS A PROMISE

"Banjo, BEHIND YOU," yelled Lee. "HEADS UP!"

In an instant Banjo spun around and fired two shots with the new Paintball gun – FLASH, FLASH – Banjo hit the T-Rex that was attacking him from behind.

"Got him," said Banjo. The T-Rex vanished into the air.

"Good shooting," said Zinzu. "You are getting much better at handling these weapons." Zinzu had set up a practice area on deck three of the starship to train the Science Team on the safe use of the new Paintball guns.

It was like a video game, but the boys were actually inside the game. "Banjo, always remember," continued Zinzu, "to raise the barrel of your gun up in the air when someone runs in front of you so you do not shoot them by mistake. Do you understand?"

"Okay, I keep forgetting that," said Banjo. "I'll work on it."

"Yeah," agreed Lee, "earlier you almost shot me in the head, TWICE!"

"All right pay attention … here is the next practice," said Zinzu, as he pushed some buttons on a computer. The space around Lee and Banjo instantly turned into a dense green jungle.

"Awesome, this looks and feels totally real," whispered Banjo.

"Yeah," answered Lee, "it even has smells, too. That is scary real."

The boys sneaked through the jungle with their Paintball guns ready.

"SQUAK," a sound came from their right. The boys turned and aimed their guns into the jungle. They waited, but nothing happened. They kept on walking and walking and walking, but still nothing attacked.

"Not knowing when or where they are going to attack us is driving me nuts!" whispered Lee.

"Me, too," said Banjo. "Stay on red alert."

Zinzu let the boys walk a little longer, until he saw them starting to relax a little. That is when he sprung his trap. He quietly pushed a button on the computer.

"SCREEETCH," without warning three small meat-eaters covered with feathers leaped from the trees above and came straight at Lee and Banjo.

FLASH, FLASH, FLASH – Lee shot the first dinosaur while Banjo shot the other two – POOF – the dinosaurs vanished.

"Whoa! That was a close one!" said Lee.

"Those were Birdosaurs," said Banjo. "They were so life-like it was freaky!"

But Lee and Banjo did not see the fourth and fifth Birdosaurs that were attacking them from behind.

"SCREEETCH," went the Birdosaurs and – FLASH, FLASH – the Birdosaurs vanished.

The boys ducked. "HEY, who shot?" asked Banjo.

"Not me," answered Lee.

"You guys missed a couple," said a voice at the edge of the practice field. "You were almost Birdosaur food, again."

"Excellent shooting, Samantha!" exclaimed Zinzu, clapping his hands.

"Thanks," replied Sam. "These Paintball guns make it so much easier to hit stuff. They are much better than the sling shots we were using. Is it okay if I join the practice?"

"Of course," replied Zinzu. "Now boys, you must remember that many dinosaurs hunt in packs and will attack from the front AND the back. You must be more alert. Let us try that practice again. Here we go ..."

Back on the bridge, Arbee and Dino were discussing the history of Chow Chow dogs.

"Hmmm," thought Arbee. "The computer says that

Chow Chows are one of the oldest dog breeds on Earth. Is that correct?"

"Yes, I guess," thought Dino. "My ancestors come from ancient wolves, from a big place called ... China I think."

"And the ancient Chinese people used Chow Chows as guard dogs," thought Arbee, "and, it says here, they used them as war dogs as well. Is that right?"

"Yes, Chows are good guard dogs," thought Dino, "and we used to fight in wars, too. You see, Chow Chows used to be a lot bigger and meaner than we are now, but that was a long time ago."

"I see here also that they used them to pull carts," thought Arbee, "and is it really true that people in the past used Chow Chow dogs for ... FOOD and used their ... SKINS also for clothes?"

"Yes, they did," answered Dino. "That's why we Chow dogs do not trust people."

"Interesting," thought Arbee. "Please explain."

"Okay. Chow dogs will only be close to ONE person, once we have made sure we can trust them," thought Dino, "and when we are sure that they are not going to hurt us or eat us."

"So that is why Chow Chows are not close to their owners like other dogs," thought Arbee. "That's why you are so independent. So, are they a little like cats?"

"CATS?" thought Dino. "Chows Chows are NOT like CATS!"

"Oh, I apologize," thought Arbee. "Let us just say Chow Chow dogs are very independent dogs."

"Okay, that's better," thought Dino, as he let out a snort.

"Tell me, are you close to Banjo or anyone in his family?" thought Arbee.

"I am close to Banjo and a little with his dad but I am not very close with the rest of his family," answered Dino. "But I will protect them because they are part of the family I belong to."

"So, Chow Chows can CHOOSE who they are loyal to and who they protect. Am I right?" asked Arbee.

"Yes we can," he answered. "Chow dogs make up their own minds."

"All right then, Dino, I want to make an agreement with you," thought Arbee. "I want you to agree to STAY WITH THE SCIENCE TEAM AT ALL TIMES and protect them. And, if you promise NEVER to run off chasing things, I will tell Banjo not to put a leash on you. What do you think about that?" asked Arbee.

Dino thought for a moment. "No leash, huh, and what if I do not keep the promise and I go chase something?"

"Then I will have to ask you to leave the Science Team and stay home," thought Arbee. "I cannot allow you to put yourself or the Science Team in danger by running off to chase things."

"I know you love to chase things," Arbee continued,

"but I am asking you to change your JOB as a dog from ... protecting by CHASING to ... protecting by STAYING and DEFENDING. What do you say, can you do that?"

Dino sighed as he thought it over. "Okay, I agree. I will do that," he thought. "I will stay and protect the Science Team and not run off chasing things."

"Do you promise to do this?" asked Arbee.

"Yeah, I promise to do that," answered Dino. "I give you my word as a Chow Chow."

"Excellent," thought Arbee. "Let us complete the agreement with an old Earth custom, a hand shake, or paw shake."

Dino raised his paw to Arbee's hand and they shook. "Thanks, Arbee. Thanks for helping me and listening to me and not for hitting me with a rolled-up newspaper."

"I consider you a very good friend," thought Arbee, "and an important part of our team. You are very brave."

Arbee floated down and gave Dino a hug.

Dino licked Arbee's face and wagged his tail. He was happy again because dogs, like people, want to work and help, but they need to know what they are supposed to do.

"Are you sure this is a good idea?" asked Banjo. "I mean, Dino without a leash?"

"I think you are making a huge mistake, Arbee," said Lee.

"Dino and I have an agreement that he will stay and protect the team," said Arbee. "That is his new job. Right, Dino?"

"WOOF!" barked Dino. "We have got an agreement," he thought. "We even shook hands on it. So shut up, you pesky little kids."

Dino, Arbee, Sam, Lee and Banjo had returned to the valley and were now standing next to the herd of Stegosaurs. Zinzu and Bootsey had remained aboard the starship to take care of things there.

"Finally," sighed Arbee. "My research is moving along again. What a week it has been."

Lee and Banjo were standing guard, keeping a sharp eye out for meat-eaters with their new Paintball guns.

Dino was staying close to Banjo, keeping his distance from the Stegosaurs so he would not be mistaken for one of their babies again. He was watching two Allosaurs off in the distance. "Gerrrr woof!" he growled. "Hey, Banjo, watch the edge of the forest," he thought, "bird-lizards over there."

"I see them, Dino," said Banjo, as he looked where Dino was looking. "Lee, heads up, there are two Allosaurs over there."

"I see them," answered Lee. "They are pretty far away, but they could be trouble."

"Samantha, have you finished recording the high and low-pitched sounds that the Stegosaurs have been making over the last day?" asked Arbee.

"I think so," she replied. "I have recorded over twenty different calls so far, but I think there are more."

"That is quite all right," said Arbee. "Hand me the recorder computer and we shall see what some of these different sounds mean to our Stegosaurus friends."

Arbee took the recorder from Sam. No one could hear the sounds that Sam recorded except Dino and the Stegosaurs, but by looking at the computer's screen Arbee could pick up and play one of the sounds. He picked a sound, pushed a button, and played it so some of the dinosaurs could hear it. At first nothing happened, but then some of the Stegosaurs began walking forward.

"Ah, ha!" said Arbee. "That sound means 'move forward' so let us try another." He pushed a button and played another sound. This time some of the Stegosaurs turned around and walked the other way.

"Good. Now we are getting somewhere," said Arbee. "That sound means 'turn around and walk the other way'."

"It's like a language," said Sam.

"It certainly is, Samantha!" exclaimed Arbee. "It is dinosaur-speak."

"Just don't play the 'attack the Science Team' sound," said Lee. "We have had enough dinosaur attacks for this week."

Arbee tried another sound and "EERRRRRAHHH!" Some of the Stegosaurs began raising their tails and rattling their plates. Their fins began to turn bright red. Everyone except Arbee quickly backed away from the angry animals.

"Whoa, ARBEE!" yelled Lee. "TURN THAT OFF!"

Arbee turned the sound off and the Stegosaurs calmed down.

"Well," said Arbee, "that was most interesting indeed."

"Should we be doing this?" mumbled Lee. "I really don't think we should be doing this."

Arbee played through all the sounds while Sam noted down what the Stegosaurs did when they heard them.

They also discovered that different groups of Stegosaurs in the herd used different sounds for different reasons like when the mothers talked to their babies.

"It is amazing how well they work together," said Arbee.

"It is like I said," thought Dino. "A bunch of not-so-smart animals working together to be smarter."

"Right you are, Dino," thought Arbee to Dino.

"This is awesome stuff paleontologists could never find out unless they were here," said Banjo.

Sam was feeding one of the older Stegosaurs, who seemed happy to have the help. "Hey, Banjo, check out this guy's skin," she said. "You should put this in your notes."

Banjo moved closer, very slowly, and lightly petted the dinosaur's skin. "It's kind of like a bumpy elephant skin, not a scaly reptile skin."

"I would not be doing that," thought Dino. "That thing

might adopt you and you will have to eat yucky plants for the rest of your life. Oh, and have fun trying to sleep at night with all their snoring."

"Arbee, this is Zinzu. Come in, urgent!" a call came to Arbee from the starship.

"Arbee here, go ahead."

"I am tracking a large space ship flying directly toward Earth," said Zinzu.

"Is it Captain Greck's ship?" asked Arbee.

"No, it is not," replied Zinzu. "Greck's ship left this solar system quite some time ago. This ship has no identifying markings. I suspect that it is a pirate ship." Piracy was a serious problem for civilizations in this time period.

"Blasted pirates!" cursed Arbee. "Zinzu, prepare for immediate departure, Arbee out."

"The ship will be ready for departure when you arrive, Zinzu out."

"Science Team, we must leave at once," ordered Arbee. "Get back to the shuttle and quickly!"

"Space pirates and Space civilizations!" complained Lee. "This isn't supposed to be happening."

"Yeah, we sure didn't learn about THIS in history class!" said Banjo.

"Bye, Stegos," Sam sighed as she petted one of the dinosaurs on the nose. "It was nice to meet you, but we have got to go now. Watch out for the space pirates. Okay?"

Everyone started running back to the shuttle, jumping over rocks, bushes and logs trying not to trip. Arbee flew ahead to open the shuttle's hatch and prepare for take off. He was on board in an instant.

Lee, Banjo, Sam and Dino were almost to the shuttle when, without warning, the pack of Allosaurs that had been hiding at the edge of the forest came running after them, thinking they were food.

"Hey, guys, look out," yelled Lee, "ALLOSAURS!"

Sam, Lee and Banjo quickly formed a defensive line, exactly like they were taught to do by Zinzu. Dino stayed close to the team and barked, just as he promised Arbee.

The team raised their paintball guns and ...

"Ready," commanded Banjo, "aim ... FIRE!"

BAP, BAP, BAP, BAP, BAP and –FLASH – the Allosaurs did not have a chance. They were hit with a shower of flash marbles from the Paintball guns. The dinosaurs dropped to the ground – THUMP, THUMP – like rocks.

"Banjo ... this ... is ... awesome!" gasped Lee. "I love these things."

"Come on!" yelled Lee. "Get in the shuttle, quick!"

They leapt into the shuttle. Banjo closed the door while Sam helped Arbee with the controls.

"Everyone is on board, including Dino," said Lee. "We are ready to go."

"We are off," said Arbee.

The shuttle rocketed into the sky and was gone.

Once back at the starship, Arbee took everyone directly to the time tunnel entrance. "Sorry to cut this short," he said. "Turn in your Paintball guns, please, and off you go."

"Arbee, what if you and Zinzu get attacked by the pirates? How will we know if you're okay?" asked Sam.

"We will be fine," answered Arbee. "Zinzu and I have been trained in the Library Service to handle these sorts of things and we have dealt with these hazards before. Check back with me in a few days Sam. Lee, Banjo, I will see you in two weeks."

Arbee floated over to Dino. "I see you stuck by the team," he thought to Dino. "Well done. You kept your promise. Now that was not so hard, was it?"

"No, I just needed to know what to do," thought Dino wagging his tail. "Thanks, Arbee. See you next time."

"Yes, next time for sure," thought Arbee.

One by one, the team dove into the tunnel and were gone in a flash.

Sometime in the Future
Somewhere in the Western U.S.

In a poorly lit basement beneath the Museum of Natural History, a team of paleontologists, students and some volunteers were hard at work cleaning a newly arrived shipment of fossils from somewhere in the state of Colorado, U. S. A.

The sound of hammers, chisels, drills and other tools filled the room and dust floated through the cold air.

One fossil in particular was a very rare find. It was an almost complete, perfectly preserved skull belonging to an adult Allosaurus.

They were in the final stages of cleaning it when one of the students noticed something odd. He cleaned off more rock from an area on the side of the skull.

"Dr. Clark, sir," said the student. "Dr. Clark, you might want to take a look at this."

Dr. Thomas Clark, who was head of the Department of Paleontology at the museum, stopped what he was working on and walked over to the table where the student was working on the skull.

"You didn't break it, did you?" asked the doctor jokingly.

"No ... oh no, sir ... I didn't break it," replied the nervous student.

"Relax, kid. I'm kidding," said the doctor as he smiled.

"What do you want to show me?"

"This right here," replied the student. He showed the doctor a perfect two inch hole going through both sides of the dinosaur's skull.

"Hmmm!" grunted Dr. Clark as he looked it over. He grabbed a metal rod from a nearby work table and put it through the holes. "It's perfect. It goes straight through. Well that's pretty weird."

By this time, Dr. Clark's assistant, Jeff, had wandered over to see for himself what was going on.

"I have never seen anything quite like it. This must have happened somehow during fossilization," mumbled Clark. "Maybe it's a birth defect or something, who knows ... pretty strange ..."

"Nope, that is not the reason," said Jeff, "but I know what did cause it." Jeff put his finger into one of the holes. "See the clean, sharp edges of these holes, Dr. Clark?"

"Yeah," replied Clark, "I see the edges. What about it?"

The others in the work area had also gathered around to see the strange holes in the skull, mumbling to each other.

Jeff stood back and in a loud voice announced, "This hole was burned through and it is not a birth defect. This Allosaurus was shot through the head with some sort of … laser gun … by ancient aliens."

Everyone turned to look at Jeff like he was crazy.

Jeff tried to keep a straight face. He finally burst into laughter and soon everyone was laughing.

"Aliens," Dr. Clark said. "Ha, ha, haa, that's a good one. All right, the comedy show is over. Everybody get back to work."

MAP OF STEGOSAURUS VALLEY

Arbee's time traveling Star Ship

where we were attacked by Birdosaurs

STEGOSAURUS VALLEY

FOREST

where Dino and Teeg were trapped in the Stego herd!

where Dino chased the Birdosaurus into the forest

This is Arbee's ship disguised as a big stego!

Lots of Allosaurs in here

This is where we let Teeg go back to his ship.

Swamp

By-
Banjo Montgomery,
Lee Wong,
Samantha Berk,
Dino (Dinosaur Dog) and
Bootsey (the cat).

Captain Greck.

Captain Greck's Star Ship.

Made in the USA
San Bernardino, CA
16 February 2017